AF444275

DON'T PULL OUT

Seven Erotic Stories

MAYA K. CHASE
mayakchase@gmail.com

IN THE *DON'T PULL OUT* COLLECTION
By Maya Katherine Chase

MY
NAUGHTY
PROFESSOR
Lockdown Lovers
MAYA CHASE

My alarm sounded, my phone buzzing itself across my bedside table and onto the floor, falling screen-side down into a pool of morning sunlight. It was 9:27. I'll admit, I cut it pretty close when it comes to morning classes, and since BU went online I've been cutting it even closer. I threw the comforter off, and sat up at the edge of the bed.

I let the alarm buzz, my brain catching up to the clock.

Bending over and planting my feet squarely on the carpet I picked up my phone and turned it off.

The room was quiet, and I think I was the only one awake in the whole house. My parents and sister wouldn't be up for another hour. I looked around, my eyes shedding their sleepy haze and taking in my childhood bedroom: a poster of Shakira I'd had since middle school, a Frisbee I'd won in a rec tournament just last January, sophomore year of college, a bag full of old shirts set aside for donation. The room had blue curtains that I'd picked out years ago, and a blue shag carpet over oak floorboards. Speckles of dust floated in the morning rays, dancing through the air, and making my old bedroom look almost like a painting, or a cartoon. It was warm. I stretched, and closed my eyes, and yawned, and realized I had already wasted too much time. I was late to class.

Professor Isabella Camero's Spanish class started at 9:30 precisely, and she perhaps cared way too much about punctuality given the circumstances we were all going through. It was 9:33 by the time I'd fumbled for my MacBook under the bed, adjusted the pillows, and sat back down in bed. I pulled the thick down comforter over my bulging morning wood, trying to ignore it, and clicked on Zoom. Video: off. Microphone: muted. Professor Camero was mid-sentence— *"y entonces cada grupo va a preparar una presentación para la classé..."*

I yawned, not paying attention. My eyes had slipped closed, dreams seeping in at the corners. Thoughts of the girls in my class who I'd flirted with until we had to leave campus.

"Kyle? I'm so glad you joined us. I'll note the time." Camero spoke in English, startling my foggy brain and bringing me back to the moment, to the screen. I looked up. My professor was looking right at me, it seemed, through the camera. Her lips were pursed, her dark hair pulled back into a ponytail. She was teaching from her bedroom in a red tank top — I could see the unmade sheets behind her bare shoulders. I wished the camera cut off just a little bit lower, so I could see more of her. She seemed to be waiting for me to respond. "Kyle, can you turn on your mic and let me know you're paying attention?"

"Yeah, I'm here," I said, my voice still gravelly from sleep. It was a small class of eight people, so she was more than willing to hold things up for me. "Morning, Professor."

"Gracias, Kyle. Stay after class for a minute and we'll chat, you can't keep showing up late like this, we're in the same time zone. *Continuemos—"*

I was wide awake, now that I'd been called out, and honestly watching her toss her hair every once in a while and surreptitiously adjust her tank top kept me hard. I never had a chance to deal with my morning wood on 9:30 class days. Sure, I could wake up earlier, but who wants to do that? I just put my MacBook on my lap, holding everything in place and trying to ignore it. But not today. Usually, I was too sleepy to pay attention, and my grades were no doubt slipping in Camero's class as a result — most days I wasn't keyed in, watching her every move on the screen, listening to her song-like Spanish voice.

I cannot lie. I've fantasized about her. In class — when we were still on campus — sometimes I'd pay more attention to her body than to what she was saying. That's part of why I'm so bad at Spanish. Now, lying in bed, still naked from the night, I could feel my cock twitching, pressed down by my laptop. I watched her plump lips form careful letters: *"intenta, ahora classe."* When she adjusted her seat and pulled back from the camera my cock pulsed as I watched her large breasts bounce.

Fuck. I couldn't resist this. I shoved my hand under the covers and clutched my cock, feeling the blood rushing through the shaft. I knew I shouldn't watch her like this. Maybe a quick release and I can focus, I thought.

I swiped away from Zoom and opened a new tab on my browser. *Professor student porn*, I Googled. I could feel the heat building behind my groin. Moving the laptop I spread out on my bed, crooking a knee to better grip my cock. I imagined Professor Camero surveying my body — I knew I wasn't bad looking. Would she compliment my broad shoulders and muscular chest, or would her eyes stray right to my cock? I pretended the Spanish words she spoke were words for me — "Fuck me, Kyle."

On the screen I found a classic scenario, one I wanted to *be in* right now. The professor was a horny looking man in his thirties, loose buttoned shirt and glasses he would definitely take off in a minute or two. The girl was a big-breasted blonde in booty shorts, her tanned legs ending in black high-heels. Fuck, I'd hit that.

"I'm afraid I'll have to fail you, Jane," the professor said, putting his hand on her shoulder and stroking her neck. "Unless we can come to some other sort of arrangement."

"Anything you say, Mr. Henderson," she said. She began to unbutton her short white shirt. "Would this work?"

She wasn't wearing anything underneath, and I drew a quick breath as her breasts heaved out. This would never happen, right? Or could it. I'd heard so many stories floating around of secret liaisons with professors. Freshmen girls going over for dinner to their professor's apartment: "I've never met a student as bright as you," I imaged them saying, before seducing them onto the couch. "I want to show you something." My mind couldn't hold on to one thought for more than a moment, but at least my hand was steady, stroking my cock slowly.

The girl had her professor's cock in her mouth. He sat on a shitty metal desk, some prop pulled out for the scene.

"Mmm, so big," she said, the sweet, wet sound of her sucking filling my headphones. "If I let you fuck me, will I get an A?" She asked. The camera zoomed in on her face, the professor's first load of cum slipping from her lips. "I don't want this to end."

"Bend over, and I'll see what I can do," he said. The video was too quick, cutting between the professor's long strokes into her pussy and her face as she cried out for more. She gripped the desk she'd been bent over with both hands, arching her back and offering herself fully to him.

"Fuck," I moaned, rubbing my cock faster. "Oh, fuck."

Though the roles were reversed, I imagined myself pounding into Professor Camero like that. Her thick, Spanish legs spread out in front of me, her pussy dripping and her cries filling the room.

I heard my name over the girl's cries and the slap of her professor's balls against her groin.

"*¿Kyle? ¿Qué piensas de eso?*" I slammed the pause button faster than anything in my life and my fantasy crashed to a halt. My blood was pumping and I was still rubbing my cock with the intention to fill up Camero's tight pussy. What had I missed? I hadn't accidentally turned on my video, right? I worried. I clicked back to Zoom. No, my video was still off.

Play it cool, Kyle, I told myself. But I was breathing like I'd been fucking.

I clicked on the microphone.

"Sorry, Professor, what did I miss I was in the bathroom for a minute." My words trembled through the obvious lie.

"I was just assigning groups, Kyle. I put you with Meg for the final project. Is that okay?" She broke into English and didn't bother acknowledging my disobedience.

"Sure," I said.

"*Muy bueno.*" She was about to go back to teaching, but paused a moment longer on my disruption. "And Kyle? I'm really going to need to speak to you after class, this is unacceptable."

"Okay. Sorry, Professor."

"Now, *presta atencion.*"

My cock throbbed, still unsatisfied, and my heart beat hard in my chest. I felt like I'd almost been caught. I knew that was impossible, since the video and audio were both turned off, but it felt like a close call nonetheless. There on my screen the professor's cock was buried balls deep in his student's pink pussy, but I was too afraid to click play. I held my cock tight, and sighed automatically. I closed the tab and tried to pay attention in class, but my mind was still caught between fantasy and the fear of being found out.

Class ended shortly, and I was going to sign off. I'd already switched from graded to pass-fail and didn't really feel like sticking around to get talked at by my angry professor, especially since I was still rock hard and she was still smoking hot. She got to me before I could leave.

"*Adios, classe!* Kyle, remember we need to talk after class. Stick around."

"Alright, Professor," I said, cornered. I lay on my bed, the laptop at arm's reach in front of me. The other students left the virtual classroom, a little ding following each, and soon just Professor Camero and I were left.

"Kyle," she said. It felt like she was looking right at me, even with the video off. Hers was the only video on the screen, now. We were alone. "Can you turn on your camera so we can talk like adults? I'm pretty disappointed with your performance recently."

"I'm still in bed, actually, Professor." I said, turning my audio on permanently but not my video.

"That's ok, we need to chat face-to-face. This is serious." She was annoyed. I could see it in the way she shifted in her seat. The problem was, I was still hard as a rock and was only turned on more the more frustrated she became, the more she focused her attention on me. "You haven't really participated for weeks, Kyle, and you've been late almost every day. I know you've probably put this course to pass-fail, so maybe it will help you if I tell you that currently, you're on the edge of failing." She paused. "Kyle, please turn on the video so I can see your face."

"Okay," I said. The moment from the scene earlier flashed through my mind. *I'm afraid I'll have to fail you…* I turned the video on, not bothering to cover up. *Some sort of other arrangement.*

"Oh—" There was an awkward pause as Professor Camero stopped mid-sentence. "Kyle maybe you should—"

"Sorry, I said I was in bed." I said, smirking a little bit. I could see she'd gone red, even through the screen. I rushed on: "I'm late to class because I oversleep, sorry about that. I'll try harder to participate, just please don't fail me. I'm having a *hard* time."

"I…" She stumbled over her words. "Sorry, it's hard to concentrate, Kyle. This isn't professional."

"I'll cover up." I said. "But, could we work something out about me failing?" I reached for the comforter.

"Wait."

"Yeah?"

"I've always wondered what you looked like… lq ike this."

"Naked?"

"I know it's not my place…" She moved a hand to her lips instinctively.

"No, it's fine." I laughed. Her tone had shifted from one of annoyance to one of seductress. "I'm obviously turned on, too." I took a chance and wrapped my hand around my cock. I stroked it, just a little.

"You're a very good looking guy, Kyle," she said.

"Well, you're a pretty hot woman yourself, Professor Camero," I said. I squeezed my cock harder, moving just a little closer to the camera.

"Please, call me Isabella."

I hesitated. It was all or nothing now, though.

"Ok, Isabella," I said. "Do you still think I'm going to fail your class, or can figure out another sort of arrangement?"

This was really happening! My heart was pounding. She could turn me in at any minute. Or another student could log back on, and it would all be over.

"I… think we can work something out."

"I like the sound of that," I said.

"Kyle… I've never done this before." She paused
again, her wide eyes looking through the screen to mine.
"At least, not with a student. I mean, I've stripped on cam
before… and…"

"I've never done this with a professor before," I
said. I chuckled. She laughed, too, and the tension eased a
bit. "I'm all yours."

"So," she said, seizing the moment now. "You'll do
anything for me? Anything not to fail?"

"Anything," I said.

"You'll talk me through what you'd do to me? If
you were here?" She started to remove her top. From under
the red tank top her large, cute breasts emerged. When it
was completely off, she sat topless in front of her webcam,
teasing me. She pressed a thumb onto one nipple, rubbing it
softly in a circle. I gripped my cock harder, rubbing up and
down, my pulse quickening still.

"I'd strip you down," I said. I ran my hand across
my abs, past my cock, tempting her. I cupped my balls.
"That's what I'd do first, Isabella." She seemed to get off
on me using her first name, almost as if it were forbidden.

"I'd make you eat my pussy, then," she said, biting
on her index finger and making eye contact with me. Even
through Zoom I could see how deep and innocent her big
brown eyes really were.

"I'd love that," I said. "I bet you taste so sweet,
Professor."

"Isabella." She smiled.

"I bet you taste so good, Isabella."

"Now say it in Spanish you naughty boy," she
cooed. She dropped her hand from her breast and picked up
her laptop, moving to the bed and lying down much as I
had done. I could see she only wore a thin, black thong.
She reached a hand under the waistband and moved her
forefinger over her clit.

"You lectured in a thong," I said, almost laughing, breathless. I slowly moved my hand up the shaft of my cock, putting on a little show. "That's so hot."

"Why not?" She smiled, adjusting the camera so I had a better view of her legs. "Don't want to cover these up, do I?"

"No…" I said.

"No is right." She let out a short breath. "You're a very bad boy, Kyle. A bad student and a bad boy. Now eat my pussy in Spanish or I'll fail you." She closed her eyes, rubbing circles on her clit, her leg twitching. I struggled to find the right words.

"*Quiero comerte la concha*," I said, the words falling from my tongue before I knew what they were.

She gasped.

"*Que bueno, Kyle*," she said. "*¡Que bueno¡*"

"*Estas muy guapa, Isabella,*" I said. "*Tengas una coño muy dulce.*"

She laughed, opening her eyes, and spreading her legs further.

"You're not bad at Spanish, really," she laughed. "And you're fucking hot… you really should try harder in class…"

"Should I keep going?" I asked. It turned me on to watch her masturbate. I worked harder on my cock the steadier she went.

"Please," she said, smiling at me. "You've got such a big cock, Kyle, I really can't believe it…"

"I'd fill up your tight pussy with it," I said before I could stop myself. "If you'd let me."

"I'd let you," she moaned, closing her eyes again. "I can't keep my eyes open," she laughed.

"Don't," I said. "Let me tell you what I'd do to you."

I could feel myself getting close, the thrill of showing off in front of my teacher ramping up the heat in my groin to a whole new level.

"What would you do to me, Kyle?"

"I'd lay you down on that bed, like you are now," I said. "Spread your legs."

She spread her legs, instinctively following my command.

"I'd kiss your sweet pussy until you're nice and wet and ready for me," I said, moaning, grasping my hard cock in both hands. "When you're ready I'd push your legs back…"

"Oh, Kyle!" She cried out, still steadily circling her clit. "Oh!"

"You have such great thighs, Isabella," I said. "Fuck, you're so fucking hot."

"Oh, you are, too, you naughty boy," she said between breaths. "You are, too. Now tell me how you'd fill me up, you've got me so so close."

"I'd push your legs back," I continued. "I'd hold onto your thighs, and spread you wide open."

"Yes!"

"Should I push right in?"

"Yes!"

"I'd push you open with my cock," I said. "You'd be so wet, and I'd slide right inside you."

"You would…" She moaned, opening her eyes again and looking at me. "Oh! That *is* a massive cock, Kyle. I don't think I can fail a guy with a cock like that…" And her head fell back on the bed again. I couldn't take my eyes off her thong, her hand working magic underneath. I wanted to be inside her.

"I'd slide into your pussy until I was so deep," I murmured. "So deep you could feel me all the way up, feel me through your belly."

"Oh!"

"Yes, I'd fuck you like that Isabella. Legs back on the bed, like that." My mind had gotten even foggier, chemicals pushing through my blood brain barrier and crippling my reason. All I wanted was her, her soft pussy filled with my cock.

"I'm so close, Kyle," she moaned. "So close."

"I'll keep your pussy stuffed full," I moaned. "I'll hold your legs back and pound you harder than ever before. It'll hurt."

She went wild, twisting and moaning on her bed, her fingers twirling around her clit, her other hand pushing aside the thong and spreading open her labia. I could see how wet she was — she was dripping all over her fingers. She pushed two into her pussy, moaning.

"It'll hurt," I said. "It'll hurt to take such a big cock but you can do it, Isabella."

She moaned louder, uttering little cries.

"Kyle! Don't stop, Kyle," she cried. "I'm so close it hurts."

"Then fucking cum for me, Isabella," I breathed. "I'll keep you stuffed so full you'll cum all over my big cock. How d'you like that?"

"So good!"

"Should I cum in your pussy?" I begged. "Should I fill you up?"

"Yes!"

"I'll cum inside you Isabella. I'll hold you down so you can't move and I'll fill you up. So much it'll come right out of you."

"Yes!" She groaned, turning onto her back and kicking up a leg. "I'm—!" She struggled, gasping and moaning and writhing. I watched her. "I'm cumming, Kyle! I'm cumming," she cried into the camera, opening her eyes. "Give me that big cock you naughty boy. Fuck!" I saw her collapse backward onto the sheets, exhausted, and I wished

I could be there to spread her open, to feel her warm pussy around my cock, and to fill her with my cum.

"Oh, my god," I moaned. "I've gotta cum."

"Do…" She moaned. She tried to sit up, opening her eyes. "Let me watch."

"I just want to fill up your pussy," I groaned. "That's all I want."

"You can," she soothed. "You can, cum for me now Kyle."

I felt the heat rush from my balls and race through my cock. Hot cum exploded from the tip of my cock and onto my hand, my chest, the bed. Professor Camero giggled.

"That's so much!" She cried, covering her mouth. I could tell she was grinning.

I moaned, letting the rest of it flow from me, covering my hand, still moving up and down on my cock. It should have been inside her body, I thought. I hadn't taken my eyes off of her. Her round lips, her big, soft breasts, and her jet-black lacy thong. Fuck, she was the hottest woman I'd ever seen.

"I think you passed the class, Kyle," she said, smiling broadly and resting on one elbow. "Your Spanish has improved. Damn, it's too bad we don't have class in person anymore."

"Thanks, Isabella," I said, still holding my cock. "I know… That was so fucking hot. What I'd do to you in person..."

"We should do it again," she said, teasing me by squeezing a plump breast. "Tomorrow?"

"Of course."

"Don't be late!" She laughed.

MY
NAUGHTY
PROFESSOR
WANTS
MORE
Lockdown Lovers
MAYA CHASE

I want you.

It was dusk on a Saturday when I got her text. My phone buzzed and I saw Professor Isabella Camero's name flash across my screen. I was sitting at the kitchen counter, eating the last of my microwaved dinner. I put down my spoon to text back, my cock thickening instinctively in my pants.

Now? I replied.

She'd given me her number after one of our after-class video sessions. She had orgasmed as I told her exactly, exactly how I would fuck her: bent over her desk during a class with my cock buried completely in her ass. She lost it. She came and shook and told me it was beyond time she gave me her number. I punched it into my contacts and we started texting later that day. We'd trade pictures, and set up times to masturbate together over Zoom or Facetime. Sometimes, she texts a simple *Want to watch?* And I always do. I'll let her watch me, too, even if she's not doing anything herself. And we both love the thrill. Isabella is my naughty professor, and I'm her bad, bad student — and we like it that way. She texted back:

Yes, now.

What do you mean?
Get your shoes on an come fuck your teacher.
I can't! We're in lockdown.

Quarantine tho!
You'll break it for me. Now come ;)
What do you want me to do to you?
Everything. Get your shoes on or you'll have an F
on your transcript.
Omw.

I looked around the kitchen. My parents were pulling together something for the two of them to eat, and my sister was occupying herself with her iPad.

"I think I'm gonna go on a run," I said to nobody in particular. I started to get up, the wooden stool scraping against the floor with a dull sound as I did so.

"Is that safe honey?" My mom looked over, putting down the mixing spoon she had been holding and coming to the other side of the kitchen island. "You can get pretty close to people when you're running, are you sure you don't want to use the treadmill in the basement?"

"Yeah, I need some fresh air, actually," I said.

"Can I come?" My sister looked up from her iPad game. "I haven't gone running in a while. That sounds fun."

Fuck. My family was very much in the way of my plans. I needed to get out.

"I'd rather go alone, actually. I just need to clear my head."

"Okay!" She lowered her head back to her screen. It was as easy as that.

"Be careful out there, okay?" My mom opened the drawer in front of her and pulled out a red bandana. She handed it to me. "Keep this on, okay? Social distancing, safety, you know the drill."

"I'll be safe, mom," I said. Picking up my phone and shoving the bandana into my pocket I went upstairs to get changed. My heart was pounding. I was breaking curfew to go and fuck my Spanish Professor in the middle of a global crisis. Yes, I knew it was risky. But it was worth it, 100% — I needed to be balls deep in her pussy now more than ever. I pulled on a pair of basketball shorts and a decent looking tee, slid on a pair of trainers, and headed for the door.

I stopped a block from my house. I realized I didn't actually know where my professor lived. I texted her. It was an address in Back Bay, just over a mile away. I started jogging, the cool May night empty of people, even on Boston's busiest streets. It was weird.

The closer I got the harder my cock became, until it was positively visible through my shorts. On a normal day, I would worry someone would notice. Tonight, there was nobody who could notice.

Isabella lived in an upstairs apartment in a brick house several blocks from the Charles River. I rang the bell next to her red door, and ran my eyes over the facade: old brick, but not too old. There were iron shutters on the windows, painted what I could only guess was blue — I couldn't tell in the dim evening light. Inside, warm light filled the rooms, spilling out past red and white lace curtains into the street. She opened the door.

"Come in, hurry," Isabella said, ushering me into her small foyer at the base of the stairs. We stood for a moment, looking at each other. The last time I'd seen her in person had been in her classroom at BU, and I felt awkward about what we were about to do, despite having seen her naked on camera dozens of times at this point. Despite having made her come just as many times. Her eyes were the deep brown I remembered, and tonight she was wearing the same red top she'd worn the first time we'd broken the rules. It was longer than I had thought, reaching partway down her calves, covering up the fact that she only wore a white lace thong underneath.

"Wow," I said, reaching out confidently to put a hand on her hip. "You look hot, Isabella."

"Thank you, you're not looking too bad yourself tonight." She ran her fingers through my hair, testing the waters, seeing what I really felt like after all this time online.

I reached my hand a little further, finding her ass and giving her a squeeze, feeling her bare cheek beneath her top.

"We're breaking the rules," I said.

"I know."

I gripped her tighter, pulling her around until she faced the wall. She resisted slightly, but in a moment her palms were planted on the plaster. I lifted Isabella's red top, exposing her ass, and ran my fingers along the length of her thong. She sighed, spreading her legs on instinct.

Pulling her thong aside I traced the length of her pussy, reaching between her legs and drawing a line from her clit to her ass. She sighed again, and I'd already pulled out my cock, harder now than it had been in months. I moved closer, letting her feel my length between her legs.

"Fuck," I whispered. "You're already wet."

"You're already hard." She laughed, and stood up straight, turning back around to face me. "But put it away, Kyle, I have roommates." She laughed, and I went red, hurriedly shoving my cock back into my shorts. "Come upstairs, I'll show you my room."

The stairs emptied into a small living room with two couches, a TV, and a reading lamp at one end, by the windows. At the other stood a desk and a bookshelf, almost blocking the way to a modest kitchen. Beyond that, a short hallway with several doors. At the end, a bathroom. On one of the couches by the window a woman sat, knees up, reading.

"You'll be okay if we make some noise, Emily?" Isabella asked her as we came up the stairs. She was beaming, towing me as her prize.

Emily looked up.

"Yeah, I don't mind," she said, giggling and looking me up and down. For a moment her eyes alighted on my substantial bulge, the basketball shorts doing a terrible job of hiding my size. "Have fun."

Isabella pulled me down the hall and into a warmly lit room I recognized from our many chats. Her bed was there, messy as usual, and the small desk she ran her classes from.

She turned to me, her brown eyes meeting mine. Before she spoke she looked me up and down again, perhaps wondering if she was really doing this: taking her student to bed. She placed her palms on my shoulders, running her hands down my arms, squeezing my biceps. Finally, taking my hands.

"Okay," she said, letting out a breath and smiling. She knew what she was doing.

"Okay," I said, too. After a moment: "I'm really the first student you've fucked?"

"I haven't fucked you yet," she said, winking.

"Damn!" I smiled, pushing her onto the bed. "You're not getting out of this one, Professor."

"I know," she said, spreading her legs and propping herself up on her elbows. "Now eat my pussy you bad, bad boy. You can't fuck me until I'm satisfied, and I'm hungry."

She grabbed my hands, pulling me close, then taking me by the hair and pushing me to my knees before her. She brought my head between her legs in an instant, pushing aside her underwear to expose her wet, wanting pussy.

"Eat it like you promised you would," she said. "Like our fantasies, Kyle. Make me cum."

I couldn't respond, because she pressed my face against her pussy and I had no choice but to forge ahead. Isabella was sweet, and warm, and wet, and my heart pounded as I tasted her delicious pussy. She was shaved almost bare, save for a light landing strip of dark hair. I rubbed her warm, smooth thighs, and she twitched slightly at my touch. When I traced the length of her pussy with my tongue. She shivered and moaned.

"Yes, Kyle," she whispered, lacing her fingers ever tighter into my hair, holding me close between her legs.

I parted her labia with my tongue and lapped at her pussy carefully, her moans and quivers growing stronger with each pass. Moving to her clit I kissed her lightly, then harder, taking her jewel between my lips. Isabella arched her back, moaning as she held my head firmly in place. Making slow passes over her clit with my tongue I drove her further toward ecstasy. Her sweet smell grew stronger the closer she came to the edge, and her skin grew hotter under my touch. I could feel her pulse quicken with her breath, little sighs and moans of pleasure as I flicked her clit with my tongue and held her tight with my warm lips.

I was hard as a rock and desperate to fill her body with my cock, but Isabella held me still, driving herself to orgasm on my face, desperately moving to the motion of my tongue, trying to hold me tight with her thighs at the same time as letting loose, relaxing under my touch. Finally, she broke, he legs falling away and her body softening in bliss. I held my professor tightly by the hips, pressing my lips tightly to her pussy as I kept up my task. The taste of her juices had filled my mouth long ago, and her warmth surrounded me. It was my turn to keep her in position as I took her the final paces to crescendo.

Isabella bucked and sighed and yelped loudly as I circled her clit faster and with expert motion.

"Too much, Kyle, too much," she moaned. "Fuck… it's too much."

I didn't stop. She was on fire, her belly heaving, her hips warm, her legs tensing and relaxing as she crested. In a moment she was wailing and shaking, trying to break free from my grip. I held on tight, keeping up my little circles even as she cried out — "Yes! Too much, no, too much, Kyle! Yes! Oh, my god… Ah!"

Her pussy was dripping, a new hot, sweet taste in my mouth, wetter and warmer than before. I lapped her up. She was sweating lightly, her skin hot, her chest shaking, her breath rapid.

"Kyle," Isabella said, softly, between breaths. "Come up here…"

At long last I pulled back. I straightened up, standing and leaning over her. Her eyes were closed, her lips barely parted. I leaned in to kiss her, and her breath was hot.

"I want to fuck you, Isabella," I said, kissing her soft bottom lip and nibbling lightly. "I'm going to fill you up tonight."

"Yes," she whispered. "Yes, but kiss me first."

I did. I could smell her coconut shampoo on her luscious dark hair, and I knew she could taste her own sweetness on my lips. Isabella was warm, and as I wrapped my arms around her I reveled in the feeling of her: tangible, real, solid. I've missed the feeling of a real woman in my arms, ever since lockdown. And it's so sweet. Isabella was so sweet. The air around her was warm, her skin was soft. She was fully nude, and I kissed her neck, and I kissed her lips. Holding her tightly I kissed her breasts, and she sighed. I kissed my way down her body until I reached her pussy once again. I kissed along her warm thighs, squeezing her breasts and caressing her hips.

"You're so hot, Isabella," I said.

"You are, too, Kyle. You made me cum." She giggled.

"I know," I said. "Now you're going to make me cum, Isabella."

"Am I?"

"Yes," I said. "You're a *very* bad teacher."

"I'm a good teacher!" She protested. "You're a *very* bad student. So bad you have to fuck me to pass, Kyle. What a bad boy…"

She was right. I stepped out of my shorts and pulled off my shirt. Naked in front of her I looked at my professor in awe. Her skin was a golden tan, her breasts were large and plump and soft. Her wide hips beckoned me. Her pussy still dripped from what I'd done. Her lips, barely parted, let out quiet breaths, her rapture passing into woozy, dreamy rest. Her eyes were closed, and across her beautiful face her dark hair flowed, messy.

I stepped forward, my cock ready and eager and hard.

Taking Isabella's ankles in hand I pulled her closer to the edge of the bed, pushing her legs back until her knees touched her chest.

She started.

"Are you going to fuck me?" She asked softly, her eyes flitting open.

"Yes," I said, in a desperate whisper.

My cock slid easily into her pussy. Her warmth surged around my cock and my blood flowed hot under my skin, electricity racing over my body from my fingertips to my core. Isabella bucked again and gasped as my cock slowly filled her. When I was as deep as I could be, her eyes flew open.

"Oh, my god, Kyle!" She gasped.

"You're still so tight," I managed, moaning, too. "I ate you out and you're still so tight."

"It's because you're so thick, Kyle. Oh!—"

I fucked her slowly, holding her legs tight and slipping slowly in and out of her pussy. She moaned with each thrust, saying my name.

"Fuck me harder," she moaned.

The room blurred, my only sensations the hot wetness of her pussy wrapping my cock in bliss and the lustful smell of our bodies together. The yellow lamplight made the room seem boundless, and Isabella's body bouncing with my forceful thrusts made our sex seem timeless. She was soft, I was hard, and I pounded her until she was screaming, calling out my name and gripping the messy bed sheets tightly in her hands. With each long thrust she let out a loud moan.

"Kyle!"

"Fuck, Isabella, take me…" I moaned, too, forcing myself deeper, spreading her thick legs wider. "You're so hot," I groaned.

Our rhythm shook the bed, the wooden headboard crashing repeatedly against the wall, and in turn shaking the room. I was sure our cries could be heard around the block. She was loud. I fucked her harder, my cock glistening with her wetness everytime I pulled out, only to plunge back into her warmth again, struggling not to cum.

"Oh, God," I moaned. "I'm gonna cum, Isabella."

"Not yet," she cried. She moved her leg, placing a foot on my chest and pushing back. "I want you to take me from the back."

My cock slid from her pussy, the room stabilizing and the objects around me taking shape. My heart pounded. I needed to be back inside her. Isabella sat up, pushing her hair back from her face and grinning.

"You're good," she said.

"Turn around, then," I said, smiling, too.

She stood up and turned around, shaking her ass
ever so slightly, seductively. Leaning over, she placed her
hands together and bowed her head, offering herself. I
reached out to spread her ass, and with my foot I widened
her stance. Her pussy dripped still, moisture running down
her thigh.

"Fuck me, Kyle," she begged.

My cock didn't need encouragement. I spread her
wide and held her hips tight as I pushed inside her, my cock
slipping in with ease. Buried deeper than before inside her I
let out a long, loud moan. My cock pulsed, and I knew with
a few thrusts I would fill her up.

"Fuck—"

"You want to fill me up?"

"I will," I groaned.

Pulling back I plowed into her, and with each retreat
I slapped her ass. She cried out, louder than before, her
body shuddering with each impact. Inside her, my cock
kept her spread wide. Nobody I'd ever fucked had taken
my cock like she did.

With her wetness guiding my cock in and out, she
collapsed under my thrusts, her arms giving way and her
chest meeting the sheets.

"Oh, God, … Fuck," she cried. "Fuck… Kyle you
monster."

"You're *so* good," I moaned back, unrelenting in
my thrusts. I wanted her to collapse. I'd promised it would
hurt. Her face was a mixture of bliss and incomprehension
as I stuffed her again and again. "I'm going to fill you up
tonight," I groaned. "It's going to be too much for you."

I was there. My cock pulsed with heat and my abs
tensed, and I gripped my professor's wide hips even tighter,
pulling her close as I released. My cum flooded her, hot
and all-consuming.

"Ahhh!" I cried, pouring myself into her, the room
going black. The only feeling in the world was her pussy

around my cock, her ass against my hips, her body in my grasp. "Fuck—you're mine," I groaned.

I could feel the pressure intensify inside her, and she thrashed beneath me. I leaned over to hold her in place while I pulsed again, another hot burst of cum flowing into her pussy. "Oohhh," I moaned.
"Yes, Isabella."

My cum escaped around my cock, so much of it flowing out between us, covering our legs and spilling onto the bed. When I pulled out, Isabella turned around and clasped my hands, smiling a silly grin, giddy, blissful. She collapsed, sitting on the edge of the bed, and she kissed my chest as my cum ran from her pussy. I kissed her head, breathing in the sweet scent of her coconut hair mixed with our lust, our evening of passion.

"You earned it tonight," she whispered. "Fuck, that was the best sex I've had in a *long* time."

"Me, too," I said, still standing, wobbly-legged, spent. "Thank you, Professor."

She laughed at that, and her brown eyes found mine.

"You're not a bad student," she giggled. "In fact, I think I learned a thing or two tonight."

We collapsed into bed together, kissing and feeling one another's bodies. We pressed into one another for hours, forgetting the quarantine, forgetting that I'd told my parents I was only running for a little while. Forgetting the hour. She was warm, and the lamplight made both our bodies glow, our heat binding us, and our bodies twisted together under the sheets in blissful ecstasy. I'd broken the rules for her yet again.

TEMPTATION IN
QUARANTINE
Lockdown Lovers
MAYA CHASE

Temptation in Quarantine
A Friends to Lovers Threesome

My boyfriend Jason's Greenwich Village brownstone has served as a little prison for the three of us for nearly a month, our confinement slowly depleting one another's patience for board games and puzzles, draining our supply of wine, and leaving us truly too fickle for television. Rose was only meant to stay a week, spending her spring break with us and seeing me for the first time since she started her Ph.D. at Stanford last year. We would spend the time revisiting our old uptown haunts — the little bookstores we frequented in our Columbia days, and Fasano's Coffee Shop where we spent too many Saturdays sharing secrets. Now, we're all penned in. Rose didn't go back to California for fear of flying, and now there's no way she can.

At first, we laughed and joked and said what better luck could we have than to spend this time together. Jason and I had started going out after college, and he and Rose had never met. They hit it off, I'm sure in part because they knew so much about each other already from the stories I told. After a few cups of wine it was almost as if Jason had been an old friend from college, too..

I was actually grateful at first. Jason's work keeps him away so many nights that we rarely have dinner together anymore, and I got to see more of Rose than I'd expected, too. In that first week I became more and more used to the refrain, "Ladies, dinner's on." It was nice. He said it in that way which mocks propriety, luring us to the kitchen island with smells of rich cream and pancetta. I would grab Rose's arm and smile, proud to show off these little domestic moments. She'd smile, too, happy for me.

But as the weeks passed, and it's become clearer that this won't end, at least not soon, shadows have started creeping in. Anxiety. Jason wants me more than ever, but then there's Rose, sharing our house. We all want space, it seems, and there's not much of it. Two nights ago, Jason threw together a simple pizza — some ham, red sauce, basil, a few rounds of mozzarella. He called to us from the kitchen, and I stood up to go without pausing to smile at Rose. Perhaps we'd gotten used to each other's presence already.

"That smells delicious," she said, trailing me. I'm sorry to say I barely noted it. I responded absently.

"It does, doesn't it. He's a good cook."

Through the kitchen door. Jason handed me a wine glass, too full. I took it.

"Here you go, love," he said, putting on his best smile, despite the ritual of it at this point. He poured another and handed it to Rose.

"Thanks," she said, taking a long drink.

"This is what I look forward to," I said dryly, raising the glass to my lips.

"Me, too," Rose echoed.

"I guess this is getting old," said Jason.

"Sorry," I said, setting the wine down on the counter and going in for a kiss. "I'll try to be more pleasant." I looked into his eyes. They were tired, the rich blue tinted with exhaustion.

"It's okay," he said, smiling at me, his arms around my waist. "We're all tired of this. Let's do something fun tonight, spice it up."

"Okay." I could feel the tension I'd been holding in my shoulders ease up a bit. I managed a smile, taking in his beautiful face. Strong cheekbones and a kind smile. "The pizza looks great, Jason."

"It really does," added Rose. She'd finished her wine.

"I'll cut it up. Rose, need a refill?"

"Oh, I'd love one," she grinned, reaching back and releasing her bun, red hair falling over her shoulders. "Like Melanie said… you know, this is the highlight of my day."

Uncorking the bottle, Jason poured another liberal cup for Rose, and she thanked him through purple-stained lips. He took the pizza cutter from the drawer and prepared slices for the three of us, melted cheese still spreading over the edge of each piece.

"Why don't we throw on a movie," Jason suggested, placing his hand on the small of my back and guiding us toward the living room. "Something fun."

"What's fun?" I laughed, grabbing my plate before being shepherded through the door. "What's left to watch?"

"How about *Inglorious Basterds*?"

"I mean, I've seen it," said Rose, adding a second slice of pizza to her plate before following us.

"We all have, that's the fun of it," Jason pressed.

"Nah I want to watch something new." Rose's wine was half-emptied again.

"What about *Birds of Prey*?" I asked.

"The superhero movie?"

"Yeah," I said.

"Sure!" Jason clicked on the TV. "Do you know where it is?"

"Just search for it, it'll tell you what service it's on." Rose flopped down on the couch, and I sat next to her, my plate in my lap. Jason flipped through options on the TV and I took a bite of pizza. It was cheesy and delicious.

"This is *so* good," I mumbled.

"Found it."

"I haven't seen this yet," said Rose, leaning up against me. She always was a lightweight and a wine lover.

"Remember when we did movie nights with our friends in college, Melanie?"

"Yeah," I said. At Columbia a few of us would gather on Saturday nights a couple times a month to watch a double feature, usually a classic and a new release. *Some Like it Hot* and *Deadpool*.

"God, that was good. I miss Joe and Louisa the most I think. I wonder how they're doing."

"They got married." I chuckled.

"I know." She was becoming drunk. "I just always liked Joe, it's too bad, really."

"That was always pretty obvious."

"Was it?"

"Plenty," I said. "You've always been an easy read, Rose." I took another sip of wine and Jason started the film. The golden light of the Warner Bros. logo filled the room, and I felt Jason's arm slide behind my back, taking hold of my waist.

"How's the pizza?" He asked.

"It's good, now shh," I said, nudging him. Margot Robbie appeared on the screen, the movie's bright colors startling a dozing Rose.

"Wow," she said, snuggling into me the way only a tipsy best friend can. Jason had really poured too much wine. We finished our pizza and our wine and left the dishes piled on the end tables, ready to topple over, and we nestled together on our small couch under a great knit blanket the size of France.

By the time the credits rolled Rose was asleep against my shoulder and Jason was eyeing me keenly. He leaned over for a sloppy kiss, our wine-stained lips meeting with a little jolt of warmth. The TV had gone dark, its off-black light the only thing illuminating Jason's eager face. It was late.

"Jason, she's asleep I can't move her," I said, quietly, trying not to laugh. "We can't do anything. Stop looking at me like that!"

"Like what?" His face half fell.

"Like you want to fuck me right here, right now," I said, even quieter than before.

"Oh but I do," he said, moving a hand to cup a breast. He squeezed. I batted him away.

"We can't," I hushed, listening with dreadful clarity to Rose's steady breath. She murmured something, adjusting her head slightly. Her hair smelled of my shampoo.

Jason only smiled, the wine in his brain neglecting our guest, his eyes seeing only me. Finding my hand under the blanket he guided it to his lap. I could feel him stiffen.

"You sure, Mel?" He asked, quietly, tantalizing me.

"Maybe," I said, giving in a little. I looked at Rose. With each breath strands of red hair shivered in the dark. "She won't notice, right?"

"She's sound asleep," he said.

"Okay, then, you persistent man," I said, pulling back his zipper and leading his hardening cock from his pants. I traced the length of it with my thumb, my one hand not doing justice to his size. "How's that," I whispered.

"Lovely," Jason replied, kissing me on the cheek. He left the scent of wine and basil as he pulled away, leaning back against the couch in the living room night, the hum of the TV silencing whatever noise I was afraid to make. I wrapped my fingers all the way around his cock, hidden by the blanket, still worried my friend would wake up in her wine soaked haze and see what we were doing. I gripped him harder, and he let out a barely audible moan.

"Jason!" I shushed. Rose stirred. I let go of Jason's cock, my shoulders tensing automatically. She just murmured softly again, adjusting her position, flicking long red hair from her face. Asleep. Between my boyfriend and Rose in the dark I took in a deep breath.

I reached for Jason's cock again, finding it right where it was supposed to be, long and hard and warm, his soft tip dripping a little with precum. I knew he was looking at me, through the darkness, at my silhouette against the TV screen. I could smell his musk despite the blanket. It was strong tonight.

"I love you," I said softly, into the dark. I bent my neck and lay my head against his chest, and could feel his heart beating. I stroked his cock, gripping tightly, feeling his pulse quicken between my fingers and his heart race beneath my ear. "I hear your heart," I said.

"What does it sound like?"

"Like you're having a good time, you naughty boy," I said, smiling though he couldn't see me.

"I am having a good time," Jason whispered back. "I love you, too, Mel."

"We should probably stop," I said, sighing, and giving his cock one last squeeze. "We don't want to wake her."

"I know," he said, flashing a grin I could see through the blackness and sitting up to kiss me. "I'm the risk-taker here, Mel, I'm sorry."

"Don't be," I said. "I'm having fun, too."

Right on cue, Rose stirred again on my shoulder, lifting her sleepy head this time and yawning.

"Is it over?" She asked, sitting up and brushing loose strands of hair from her face.

"A while ago," I said, reaching for the lamp on the end table. I winked at Jason. "We didn't want to wake you. You passed out a bit."

"Sorry," Rose said, rubbing her eyes. "I think I had a bit too much wine. Blame your boyfriend."

"Don't worry, I will," I said. Beneath the blanket I felt Jason subtly zip his cock back into his pants, hiding our escapades away for later that evening. "He'll be hearing from me tonight."

"Just what I wanted to hear," she said, standing up. "Mind if I turn in for the night, Mel? These days just wipe you out, don't they?"

"See you in the morning then," I replied. "We've gotta find another puzzle to do. Something to fill the time."

"Well, I can always work on my coursework," she laughed.

"Or not. Goodnight, Rose." My hand still rested on Jason's bulge. I carefully removed it, hoping my dear drunk Rose wouldn't notice a thing.

"Goodnight, Rose," said Jason. "I hope you're enjoying your staycation."

"Jason, don't!"

"What?" He laughed, but Rose had left the room. The hall light clicked on, and the tap in the bathroom ran. "We have to joke about this stuff, it's wild," he said.

"Yeah, you're right." I stood up, too. I stretched, then looked at him and saw fire in his eyes. "Now shut up and take me to bed."

The walls in Jason's brownstone are thin, and Rose's room is positioned next to ours. I could hear her closing the door and flipping the lightswitch. Jason took me to bed nevertheless, his hands silently pulling the clothes from my body as we kissed, his body forcing mine to the edge of the bed, and down onto the mattress.

"Quiet," I hushed him, unbuttoning his shirt. Jason stood in front of me at the end of the bed, his knees spreading my legs and his hungry eyes devouring me.

"Don't worry, I'll be quiet," he said, reaching for my breasts with his strong hands. "I don't know if you will be, though."

"Jason!" I said, quietly, instinctively.

"I'm just saying, you're a loud one, babe." It was true. Often as he slid inside me he would have to cover my mouth, stifling my groans and cries. I blushed, smiling into his bright face and pulling my hair back into a ponytail. He pushed me down, pressing my bare back against the soft quilt and kissing my breasts. His lips were warm and soft and he traced my nipples with a skilled tongue.

"How's that?" He asked, raising his eyes to look at me.

"Wonderful." I ruffled his hair. "How long are you going to tease me, baby?"

"A while longer," he said, grinning and burying his face between my breasts again. His stubble was soft, and it didn't scratch as he nuzzled my chest, kissing my nipples and clasping my waist in his strong hands. He traced the contours of my belly with his tongue, down to the hem of my underwear.

"I love you, Mel," Jason said, taking my waistband in his teeth and pulling. He lifted my legs, guiding my underwear off with his mouth, leaving my pussy bare.

"I love you too, Jason," I said. I propped myself up on my elbows to get a better look at him. He radiated heat and sex and happiness between my legs, meeting my eyes. "Tease," I said.

With that he kissed the inside of my thigh, pecking softly at my skin, closer and closer to my pussy with each motion. I fell back on the quilt, letting him take the moment. His breath was warm, tickling my legs, and he smelled faintly still of red wine. I let out a soft moan, and felt a little pulse of warmth travel out from my core. He stopped just before reaching my clit, his soft tongue tracing the last distance between my thigh and my vagina. He lifted his head.

"Should I keep going, Mel?" He was smiling.

"Yes!" I whispered, eyes wide, begging him.

"Are you sure?" His eyes were glittering, teasing me even now, with his head barely inches from my clit.

"Didn't you hear me, you're torturing me with suspense."

"I just—" I hit him, softly, before he could finish. He feigned offense.

"Jason," I commanded in a whisper. "Eat my pussy."

He smiled and conceded, his warm lips meeting my labia, opening me with his tongue. I was wet, wetter than usual at least. Ever since the shutdown I'd been hornier than ever, aching for him whenever he made the slightest advance. I could smell my own sweetness as he lapped me up, the tingling rush of his warmth through my body tightening my muscles. I clenched my fingers, trying not to make noise. In the year we'd been dating, he'd gotten much better at eating me out, his tongue dancing across my labia, tracing the length of my pussy. He would fold his soft lips around my clit, kissing me. He would caress me with his tongue, making slow passes until I begged him to fuck me. He did now, his careful movement and soft warmth sending energy racing through my blood, heating my skin, quickening my heart. I couldn't help but moan — one little moan, nobody would hear.

"Jason," I said, panting. "Jason, please fill me up."

He kept at me with his tongue, though, and I met his mischievous eyes. He wanted to drive me to climax before he fucked me.

"Aah!" I let out a yelp when he made another careful pass over my clit, the heat of his touch pushing past by better judgement and out my throat in a short wail. I covered my mouth, eyes wide, willing him not to stop. Heat radiated from him. He held my legs wide with both hands, and I could sense the powerful scent of sex building between us. "Oh! Jason," I managed, "Please, fill me up now."

Finally he did lift his head. Sweat had begun to gather at his hairline, and I knew he was holding back. He'd wanted to fuck me since dinner.

"How do you want me?" He asked.

"Just take me." I let out a heavy breath and looped my legs around his waist, pulling him in. "Take off those pants and fuck me, Jason."

He unbuckled his belt and stepped out of his jeans, leaving them in a pile on the floor. Jason's cock was hard and eager. He stroked his length, gazing down at me with rapture. I could see he wanted to devour me.

"Closer," I begged.

"You wait," he said, resting the tip of his long cock between the lips of my pussy, making me even wetter than before. I ached for him, and he could see it in my eyes. With one hand he moved his cock to trace the full length of my pussy. He winked. I closed my eyes, shutting out the lamplight and feeling only his hand on my thigh and his cock at the entrance of my pussy, the warm air of our bedroom guarding us from everything outside ourselves. He plunged into me, squeezing my thighs with both hands as he did, and letting out a deep groan. My body parted for him, his cock sliding easily inside me, filling me up. He stayed there for a long moment, his hard cock pulsing, my pussy quickly acclimating to his presence.

Jason placed a hand on my belly. "I can feel it," he said."

"Yeah?" I pressed below my navel, and I could, too. The hard shape of his cock was there, and it hit me how truly deep inside me he was. I let out a giggle, awash with the warmth of the moment, the soft light of the room, and his powerful presence before me. "Oh my god," I said.

With that he pulled out again, almost all the way, and the smell of us filled the air. I gasped. He pushed my legs back against my chest and plunged in again with a soft thunk. And again. The quiet, rhythmic sounds of our bodies colliding filled our little room, mixed with my gasps and yelps, and his groans that matched each deep thrust.

"I love you, Jason," I said, softly, between breaths as he pounded me. "Kiss me."

He paused, leaning over me and finding my lips with his. Our tongues met, and he pressed his cock harder into my pussy, forcing hot currents of electricity through my thighs and up my chest.

"You're sweet, Mel," he said, pulling away and looking into my eyes. His are green, framed by dark brown wavy hair. I've always loved his eyes, little worlds of their own. I couldn't help but think how sexy he was, looking down at me like that, and I reached out to feel his chest. He was warm, his heart beating fast and strong. I tried to grip his taut muscles, but he just grinned and pulled back, pushing his cock deeper still inside me, retreating, and ploughing into me with full force. That almost knocked me out, and little black stars filled my field of vision.

"Ooh," I cried. "Fuck, don't stop, baby."

I unclenched one shaking hand and moved it to my clit, rubbing slowly while Jason fucked me. I've always loved how thick his cock is. He spreads me wide open when he fucks me, so much that it hurts most of the time, in a good way. I touch myself to bring myself to climax, over the pain, that sweet pain. Jason's cock fills me all the way up, all the way to my core. When he presses hard into me I can feel the soft tip of his penis all the way inside. As I touched myself I thought about that, about how that's what was happening to me at that moment. My man having pure dominion over my body. I was sweating, my back hot against the quilt.

"Should I fill you up tonight, baby?" He moaned his question. "Should I cum in that tight pussy, Mel?

"Mhm," I managed, eyes closed, focused on my own ecstasy. My fingers darted over my clit, my mind fogged by the smell of Jason mixing with my own sweat, my wetness — our heat. "Cum for me, baby," I groaned.

"Fuck," he cried softly, plunging the full length of his cock inside me again. "Fuck, that's it."

For a moment there was nothing but the darkness behind my eyelids and the firework of heat pouring from his cock, filling my pussy. My skin tingled. He pushed me over the edge.

"Stay there," I moaned. His cock pulsed, pushing more hot cum into my body. Tendrils of warmth spilled from my core through my limbs, and in a moment he was on top of me, pressed to my chest.

"I love you, Mel," he said. I barely heard him. My head was swimming. When he pulled out his cum ran out of my pussy and onto the bed.

"That's a lot," I giggled, kissing him. We kissed for a long time, and he picked me up to put me under the covers. "You're so hot," I said, dizzily.

Lying in bed we slowly came to our senses, spooning. The lamp was still on, casting dim yellow light across the room. Jason's cock pressed against my ass and he kissed my neck softly, cooing his love into my ear. He twirled my hair between his fingers, and I could feel how fast his heart still beat.

"I love you, too, Jason," I said, nuzzling my head back into him. I knew he was smiling. "Can you turn out the light, baby?"

When he flipped the switch and all was quiet I let out a long sigh, happy. These are long days, in lockdown, and you might as well be having sex. The city outside was almost silent, and that was perhaps the most striking thing of all.

I was almost asleep with Jason's arm wrapped around my chest, his hand clutching one breast for comfort, when I heard it. An indistinct buzzing, quiet, almost undetectable. It happens when you lie still for long enough, and your mind notices the little things it has tuned out until then. It's like when you notice the ticking of a clock and from that point on there's nothing more present in your mind. The buzzing sharpened, and I felt my chest grow tighter just so. Rose, I thought.

I almost laughed out loud. If I could hear her, then what must she have heard. All of it, I thought.

"Jason," I mumbled.

"Mhm?"

"Rose is jealous!" And I couldn't help but giggle quietly into his arm.

"Hm?"

"I can hear her vibrator," I said.

"Of course she's jealous," he mumbled. "You're fucking hot, Mel."

"Oh my god," I said, but a little bit of heat rose up in my core, and I knew I was blushing. Rose and I had been roommates. I won't pretend I hadn't fantasized about it.

"You are, though…" he said, trailing off.

"So are you," I said. We were quiet, then. I listened in the dark and kept still, the buzzing coming through the wall of Rose's room reaching me again. I thought I heard a muffled moan. "Do you think she's hot?" I asked.

"Who?"

"So you do then," I smirked, kissing the strong arm that lay across my body. "You know who."

"Okay," Jason said, quietly, and he kissed my back in return. "I'll admit she's pretty hot."

That made me blush even more, and I felt my arms and chest and cheeks burn all at once.

"She's probably thinking about us," I said.

"Probably," he laughed softly. "I told you, you're pretty loud."

"We're going to be here a while you know…"

"You're thinking we should spice things up?"

Through the wall I heard another moan, and maybe I imagined the yelp that followed. And maybe it was in my fantasy I heard my name. The buzzing continued. Damn thin walls. Actually a blessing, I thought.

"Yes," I said, so quietly I didn't know if Jason heard me.

That night I dreamt of waking up in Rose's bed. I dreamt I woke up naked in Rose's bed, and that Jason was there. When I woke up the next morning, I was hornier than ever.

Another day had drifted past, time in lockdown not behaving the way it's supposed to. Rose and I had put together a jigsaw puzzle of an old renaissance painting, and later I found myself staring out into the empty streets with a cup of tea and a blanket. It rained, and that made the indoors that much more cozy. After a while I noticed that Rose had sat down next to me, and was also looking out the window. It was nearing evening.

"Quiet out there," she said.

"Yeah, it's pretty weird."

"I remember this city being so busy all the time."

"It was until… this," I laughed, not meaning to.

"That's why I came to Columbia, you know?" Rose sipped her tea. "To get out of the midwest, away from the quiet and into the action."

"Yeah, those were the days," I said.

"I miss it a lot now, I guess," she went on. "But we're roommates again I suppose. In a way. I'm in your house at least. Eating your food."

We laughed together and went silent, letting the streets of Greenwich Village darken. Lights blinked on or became noticeable in the other houses, and blocks away the bright lights of the skyscrapers glowed defiantly against the night.

Rose touched my arm. I looked over.

"I'm glad you let me stay, Mel," she said.

"Of course."

"I would hate to be alone in California right now, and you've always been there for me. I really do appreciate it."

"Like I said, of course, Rose. You're more than just a friend. We were roommates."

"Four years," she said.

"I know," I laughed. "Those were the days, you're right. Damn, what I'd do for a bit of normal right now."

Soon enough Jason called for us. Dinner.

"I should be doing more to help," Rose said as we made our way to the kitchen. "I feel like a leech just eating your boyfriend's cooking."

"You do the dishes," I said, squeezing her arm. "It's alright."

The kitchen was warm and bright and smelled like sweet onions.

"What's cookin'?" I asked, exchanging my teacup for the wine glass Jason offered me. I gave him a kiss on the lips, holding him there for a moment. I felt the warmth from the night before rush into my chest. My eyes were closed, but I knew Rose blushed, too.

"Stir fry," Jason said when I released him. "Serve yourself a plate and we can find something fun to do tonight."

I did, and so did Rose. He'd grilled chicken and mixed it with some delicious dark sauce, sweet onions, the last of the peppers, and something I couldn't identify off the top of my head.

"Cabbage," he said.

"Really?" Asked Rose.

"Really."

"It's very good," I said, giving my boyfriend another kiss. "Delicious."

"Should we watch something?" Jason asked, topping off our wine glasses.

"Why not," said Rose.

Nestling onto our small New York couch Jason flicked through the menus until we came to the *Twilight Zone*.

"I used to watch this as a kid," Rose said.

"Me, too," said Jason. He clicked on a random episode. Rod Serling introduced the episode, about a godlike devil boy who made things disappear. We watched another, and Jason got up to refill our wine glasses a third time. We watched another one, and Rose had leaned up against me, her bright red hair a mess over my shoulder, her eyes glued to the screen and her wine glass clasped between both hands, resting on my knee.

"I could watch these all night," Rose said, her words slowed by wine. "Here, share some of that blanket." She motioned to the large knit spread that covered Jason and half of me. I pulled it over, and she finished her glass of wine, setting it on the end table before wrapping herself in the cloth and cuddling up against me. She was warm, and again I felt a hot little jolt in my chest.

"Thanks, Mel," she said. Jason clicked to the next episode. It got late. We were all drunk.

When Jason finally clicked off the TV Rose was nestled into me, and I was nestled into Jason. It was dark, and my mind felt fuzzy.

"Mel," Jason said in a loud whisper.

"Yeah."

"Mel, I'm so into you babe."

"I know," I giggled. I squeezed his arm, and I felt him moving beneath the blanket.

"We all know," Rose mumbled.

"Hm?" I remembered that she could hear, too, and I laughed.

"Jealous?" Jason whispered. It must have been the wine.

"Maybe," she said. I lifted my arm and wrapped it around her, letting her come closer. "I mean, I can hear you at night, Mel. Both of you." She giggled like a little girl, reaching up to squeeze my breast. "Maybe I am a little bit jealous, stuck here listening to you two lovebirds go at it every night."

"I know," I laughed, the alcohol loostening me, too. "I heard you last night, too, Rose."

"You did?" She pulled her hand back, her good sense scandalized for the moment.

"We did," Jason chimed in. "I think it turned her on."

"Ooh!" Her hand returned to my breast. "Oh, did it?"

"A little," I said.

"Then kiss me, Mel."

"Jason?" My nerves twisted, conflicted. I was drawn to my friend. I needed permission.

"Go ahead," he said, taking a long sip of wine and looking on.

I turned my head and met my friend's eyes. They glistened even in the dark, catching the light of a streetlamp or another living room. They were wide, and deep, and I saw the girl I'd slept with many nights not knowing if I was the only one with heat in my chest. Now I knew I wasn't. She looked at me with the deep understanding eyes of a friend and the fiery, insatiable eyes of a lover. I leaned my head toward hers, and our foreheads met. Her skin was hot. She closed her eyes and I closed mine. Our lips met, and she tasted like red wine and something else, something sweet. Her lips were warm, electrifying. My heartbeat

quickened, and even my nose grew hot. I felt Jason begin to
lift my shirt and I didn't resist. I kept kissing Rose, and she
kissed me back. The nights in college, accidentally
spooning with her as a friend slept over and stole one of our
beds, her arm resting over my body, her breath in my ear,
our secret chats — they came rushing back to me. The
moments when her hand would brush my side, and my
heart would beat faster. Jason slid my arms out of my
sleeves, and only then did we break our kiss, to let him pull
the shirt over my head. I opened my eyes, and looking into
Rose's face I knew we were more than friends now, for
real. She smiled, her eyes and cheeks and lips beaming.

"Hey," I said. "That was good."

"Yeah," Rose said, and she dropped her eyes,
inadvertently finding my newly bare breasts. I sat topless
between my boyfriend and my best friend on our little
couch, warm and happy. Letting the moment wash over us
we didn't move for a long minute.

Jason moved first, swooping in to kiss one of my
breasts, and with a hand cup the other, covering Rose's
hand and squeezing. I moaned. They both smelled of wine,
and I probably did as well.

"How's that, baby?" Jason asked.

"So good," I said, turning my head to Rose again,
begging for a kiss. She came closer, her eyes twinkling.
Our lips met again, and she kissed me hard this time.
Passionately, in full, not holding back. She parted her lips
and with her tongue traced the outline of my mouth.

"You taste like wine, Mel," she giggled, putting her
free hand to my cheek, and returning to our kiss. I never
imagined I'd truly get to kiss her, and it was almost too
much. Too much with Jason sucking on my breast. Too
much pressed between two people I loved so deeply, one so
newly discovered — or truly, permitted. Between kisses
and bright eyes I reached for Rose's shirt, lifting it over her
head and revealing the bare chest I haven't seen since

senior year of college. Her breasts had grown slightly, and were more plump.

"You look good," I said.

"Thanks," said Rose, sheepishly looking down, but not trying to cover herself. "You look good, too, Mel." She raised her eyes to mine. "A real hottie." And to Jason: "You're lucky."

"I know," he said, lifting his head from my breast only for a moment.

"He is lucky," I go on. "You've heard how lucky he is each night haven't you, babe." I laugh, and look at Rose to see if she'd accept the pet name. She did.

"I have." She giggled, kissing my neck, her warm lips leaving purple streaks of wine across my skin. "I wish I was that lucky, babe."

"You can be," I said, tilting my head back and letting her kiss beneath my chin. "But after me."

"First dibs, huh?"

"Oh, yeah," I said. "Jason, why don't you get up and show her what you've got."

Jason's eyes lit up. This had escalated out of our control, but it was electrifying and I knew he didn't want to stop either. He detached himself from my breast and stood up, smiling, and gave one of Rose's soft breasts a friendly squeeze. "Want to see what she's been taking, Rose?"

"Yes, please," Rose said, in between kisses. She made her way down my neck and across my shoulder, to my breasts, not taking her eyes from Jason as he undid his belt buckle.

I reached out to help him loosen his pants, almost pulling off his button. The jeans fell away and my boyfriend stood before us in just his shirt, his long cock hardening in front of our eyes. Rose reached out to touch it, and Jason instinctively stepped back.

"It's ok, baby." I laughed. "Let her feel you."

Rose sat up, still leaning against me but ceasing her soft kisses for the time being. She reached out again and took hold of Jason's cock. It was hard as rock in her hand, and big, too. His raw musk was overwhelming.

"It's so big," Rose started.

"Oh, I know…" I giggled to myself remembering how jealous I'd made her last night. With the two of them entranced, I took the moment to undo the tie on my sweatpants and ease them down my legs. Naked now, I pulled the blanket around myself and watched the two of them.

"Can I kiss it?" Rose asked giddily. You'd think she'd never sucked a cock the way she was acting. I knew she had. I'd caught her more than once, though I'd quickly turned and gone.

"Please," said Jason.

Rose slid off the couch and onto the carpet, kneeling in front of my boyfriend and taking his cock first in her two hands and then between her lips. I watched, and couldn't help but spread my legs, my fingers instinctively parting my labia and feeling my wetness. I audibly moaned. Jason looked at me and smiled. I pushed myself further open, and threw back the blanket so Jason could see. He winked, and took Rose's hair in one hand, guiding his cock fully into her mouth.

Her eyes went wide as she took him. I reached out with my free hand to feel her back. I rubbed her in small circles and felt her skin get hotter and her blood pump faster the longer my boyfriend's cock was in her throat. Little fires lit across my skin as I watched them, and I could see the same for Jason as he watched me, his cock buried between my best friend's lips.

"Join us, Mel," he whispered, and I complied. Sliding off the couch I knelt next to my friend on the floor. She made room for me, and Jason's musk was more powerful than before. I leaned in to kiss around the base of his cock, making my way to his balls. I held them both in my hand for a moment before taking one in my mouth and drawing in my breath. He moaned immediately, a shudder coursing through his thighs and into his core. "Fuck, Mel," he rasped. "I love you, Mel."

Jason placed a heavy hand on my head, keeping me there with his soft, warm ball between my wine soaked lips.

"Mmm," I moaned.

In a moment Rose let Jason's cock slide from her mouth, gasping for air, and I seized the opportunity to take him myself. I pushed him onto the couch and hurriedly undid his buttons.

"Mel," he groaned, closing his eyes at my touch. "What are you gonna do to me?"

"Oh, my god," Rose said, still recovering. "Mel, oh my god his cock."

"I know," I said, giggling as I bent to kiss his shaft myself. He was wet with precum and from Rose's work, and he was throbbing hard. I took the head of his cock into my mouth and tasted him. He tasted sweet, and like musk. "Mmm," I moaned again, raising my eyes to find his were still closed.

"Ride him, Mel," Rose whispered in my ear as she reached around to cup both my breasts. I felt her warmth against my back. She'd stripped, too. Fire ripped through me at that, a shudder of heat and energy. Jason opened his eyes and I winked at him, standing over him briefly before climbing into his lap.

His eyes went wide when he realized there would be no teasing this time, and I met his shock with a sly wink.

"Help me out here, babe," I said, turning to Rose. I was positioned above Jason's hard cock, thick, dripping, and pulsing. He was frozen. Rose took my cue and grasped my hips with both hands, guiding me down. "Yes…" I moaned, throwing my head back like it was my first time.

With one hand I kept my balance and with the other I slipped my boyfriend's thick cock into my wet, eager pussy.

Jason groaned, his muscles tensing under me and his back arching against the couch.

I moaned, too, slowly taking his full length inside me until I was nestled tightly against his hips.

"My god," I whispered. I placed my hands on Jason's chest. "Come here, Rose," I managed.

Rose knelt on the couch now beside us.

"Take my hand, babe," I said, palm outstretched. She took it. "Help me ride this fat cock, Rose."

"Mel…"

"You're so hot, Rose, you have no idea."

She squeezed my hand, rising to kiss me as I rose from Jason's lap, his long cock retreating from my body.

"Down," she said, when I let him slide almost all the way out. It was a command. She smiled. I sat down, back onto Jason's cock, hard. His eyes pressed shut even more, and he instinctively reached for my breasts as he groaned. I moved one of his hands to Rose's chest, and she moaned into our kiss. She was always a caring woman, helping anyone she could — kind. And in sex, too, she was generous, guiding me up and down on Jason's cock, and kissing and caressing me. In that moment, with both their hands on my body, my lips warmed by Rose's kiss, and my pussy full of Jason's hot cock I loved them both. I remembered my dream the night before, of waking next to Rose, with Jason, and almost laughed, but couldn't. Pressed tightly together Jason and I moved to Rose's electric touch, our bodies melded together at the hip. I could feel every soft pulse of his cock as my boyfriend moved under me, and as I rode him, back and forth, grinding into his pelvis with wild ecstasy. Haze clouded my mind, from the alcohol and rhythm of my body against my boyfriend's cock.

I was dizzy, my mind at capacity. I'd lost my understanding of what was happening, and Rose's breath had become some magic, Jason's hard shaft a part of my universe.

"Rose," I said, into the spinning haze. I must have been breathing heavily, because she took my head in her hands and cradled me against her chest. Jason had pulled his cock out of me, and was saying something.

"It's okay, Mel," she said, softly. She giggled. "Jason I think you fucked her senseless, my god."

"Yeah…" I murmured, my eyes half closed. I was senseless. I lay on the couch now, legs apart, dripping wetness over the cushions. I felt Rose's fingers on my clit. She was magical, I was sure. Had I cum? Not yet, no. "I need to cum," I said. "Please…"

"You will, babe," Rose cooed. Her touch was soft. Soon it was her lips pressed against my pussy. Her tongue circled my clit with rhythmic certainty. Slowly, I was able to open my eyes. Rose knelt on the rug between my legs, red hair scattered, eyes closed. Jason knelt behind her. I opened my eyes wider. The rhythm I felt from Rose's lips — her careful caress of my clit — it was Jason's doing. He had buried his cock inside her, ploughing her gently and steadily, allowing her to eat my pussy in return.

It was a long moment before the scene made its way from my vision to my consciousness.

"Oh, my god. Rose…" I stroked my friend's hair. "Jason, oh, yes." I met his eyes. He smiled at me. His hands were planted firmly on Rose's hips, pulling her to meet his long cock with each thrust. I closed my eyes again, letting the scent of us and the heat of our bodies and sound of my boyfriend fucking my college roommate roll over me. I smelled different, after being fucked. Hotter, sharper. Rose hadn't ceased her motions on my clit, licking careful tiny circles over and over and over. She moaned into me when

Jason thrusted, her hot breath sending strands of keen fire through my core. I thought of all the nights I'd lain awake in bed at college, thinking how sweet it would be to lay with her. Now I had the chance. I felt a tightness build in my core, behind the haze on my mind, deep in my body. It built and built until it was a fire waiting to be unleashed. When Rose's tongue went round again on my clit the fire rushed out, and my back arched, and I moaned loud and long. I clenched my thighs around Rose, and I felt through her Jason's powerful thrusts, driving me further into ecstasy, to climax.

"Rose!" I shouted her name into the light show in my mind. "Yes, Rose… Jason, I'm cumming," I moaned. "Oh, my god, baby."

Rose lapped me up as I came, as I moaned in front of her. I reached out for her hair, that bright red hair I'd always loved, from the moment I'd met her. I could barely see through the tears of passion that welled in my eyes. Jason kept a steady rhythm, and I heard the smack of his hips against Rose's tight ass. Her breath grew hotter on my pussy and I knew she was close, driven to the edge by Jason's cock just as I was every night. When she came she lifted her face to me, resting her head in my lap and I stroked her hair. She groaned. She shook, sweat forming on her brow and on her chest. I wiped her forehead with my hand and leaned down to kiss her head.

"Mel," she moaned. "Mel, oh my god, this. I love this."

"Yes, Rose," I whispered, still floating in my own orgasm. "I love you, Rose."

"Oh, my god, Mel." It was all she could say as Jason fucked her through her climax, pounding her all the way to the other side, her body falling limply into mine as she attempted to hold her place. I looked at Jason. He seemed far away. He smiled at me and winked.

"Mel," he said. "Mel I'm gonna cum in Rose."

I smiled back. That's so hot, I thought. He would pump my best friend full of cum while I watched in an orgasmic daze.

"Rose," I said softly. I stroked her hair gently. She'd closed her eyes and still rested on my bare, shaking thigh. "Rose, can Jason fill you up, babe?"

"Mhm," she moaned. "Mm, yes I want that."

As far away as he seemed I could still see Jason's pupils expand and his muscles tense. His arms tightened, his hands gripping Rose's hips harder than before as he pulled her close to his pelvis, ploughing his hard cock as deep as he could. His chest drew taut, and his abs turned solid.

"Baby…" Jason groaned.

Closing his eyes he let out a long, deep moan, and I knew Rose felt it all the way inside her pussy as he pumped her full, because she grabbed my arm, squeezing tight as he held her close. She opened her eyes and looked into mine. I smiled, and she grinned a girlish happy smile in return.

In a moment Jason pulled his cock from my friend's pussy, and I helped her to sit on the couch. She slumped into me, and I turned her face toward mine for a kiss. Jason climbed slowly up next to us, exhausted, spent, and happy. He smiled at me, and kissed my lips, after which I slumped in turn on his shoulder.

"Mel," he said, quietly after a minute. "That was so fucking hot. Thank you."

"Oh my god," I murmured into him. "Oh my god it was. You fucked me so hard, Jason, and then… oh my god."

"Mmm," Rose hummed, trying to speak. "Mel, your boyfriend… is so big. Fuck, Mel…"

I don't know when we fell asleep, but I know we woke up in the morning, the three of us, curled into each

other. I suppose that night was the beginning of a new
normal.

THE BAD
CUSTOMER
MAYA CHASE

The Bad Customer

A naughty waitress taken by a handsome businessman

I rushed over to his table. It was a hot Tuesday night, so hot my boss let me wear my shortest skirt on the job. I didn't notice anything particular about him as it was a busy night, and jotted down his order with the peppy platitudes I'd learned in three years as a waitress. It was only as I turned to go and as he placed a firm hand on my thigh, holding me there, that I really looked at him.

"Wait," he said. He had deep green eyes and a shock of perfect black hair. "I want something else."

"Sorry I rushed, it's a busy night," I blurted. "What else can I get you, sir?"

Of course I'd been hit on before. Every girl has. Every waitress has. But I didn't expect — I couldn't in the least have *expected* him.

"Oh no, you got my order just fine," he said. His hand was still on my thigh, and I felt him tighten his grip, moving up my leg. "I just wanted to say I want *you*."

"Me?" I'll admit it took me a pause to realize what he was saying.

"You." He met my eyes and held my gaze before winking. He broke into a broad smile, giving my thigh one last squeeze — his hand was well under my skirt by now. "Find me after your shift," he said. "I'll wait around."

I reddened. I took him in: solid build, strong arms and powerful legs. He was waiting, waiting for me to answer him. I looked away.

"Maybe," I said. My cheeks flushed and I rushed back to the kitchen.

I had other customers, I thought. I can't entertain this. What does it say about me if I say yes? I don't even know his name — will he introduce himself properly before he fucks me? Will it hurt? He seemed like the kind of man to have a large cock, the kind of cock that hurts when he enters you. I'd have to find out, I told myself. I would regret it if I didn't, right? My pussy answered for me, getting wetter with each thought.

He was waiting at the end of my shift, just as he said he would. The night had cooled, the sun had begun to set, and he'd pulled on a leather jacket. He stood now, leaning against the hood of a black '73 Cadillac convertible smoking a Kool.

"So?" He asked, uncrossing his boots and standing straight as I approached.

"Well, I came, didn't I?" I said, meekly.

"You did." He said. "Do you want to get in?"

Shit. Was he going to kidnap me? My eyes must have gone wide, because he laughed, dropping his cigarette and stomping it out on the pavement.

"Don't worry," he said. "Tell your boss you're gonna go for a drive — give her my plate number if you want."

He was easy, friendly. Ok. I'll do this.

"I'm fine," I said, laughing lightly. "Don't you worry, you put me at ease. Where are we going?"

"Away from here." He said. Looking me over: "Somewhere you can take off that skirt."

I felt a rush in between my legs. He came forward, putting his arm around me and guiding me to the passenger door.

"Get comfortable," he said.

I climbed in, the leather seat enveloping me, warm from the day. The ignition clicked, and we peeled out of the Hanley's parking lot. Turning onto the state highway my new man took one hand off the wheel, draping his arm over my shoulders.

"So," he started, "what's your name?"

"You finally asked," I giggled. "It's Isabel. What's yours?"

"Nick," he said.

"Nice to meet you, Nick," I said. "You're a bold man, hitting up your waitress like that."

"I know," he replied. "But you seemed worth the risk, Isabel. The moment I saw your legs…"

We turned off the highway and onto a dirt track. Nick squeezed my shoulder as if to say *don't worry*, and soon enough he put the car in park in small clearing. The woods were silent but for the hoot of an owl in the distance, and I could see the stars glimmer through the gaps in the treetops. Nick left the engine running, the Cadillac's headlights filtering off into the forest.

"I think we'll be alone here," he said.

"I'd have to agree," I replied.

He opened the door, stepping out into the clearing and circling around to my side of the car.

"Come here," he said, offering his hand. I took it.

He had a firm grip, and even in the darkness I could see his eyes glimmer with desire.

In that moment my heart pounded, excitement and lust and fear and adrenaline pumping through my blood all at once.

Nick led me to the hood of the car where we finally faced each other. Both hands on my hips he held me close to his body, close enough to feel his hot breath on my forehead and his hard cock bulging in his pants.

"Can I pick you up?" He asked.

"Yes," I whispered. My heart still raced, and my pussy had only gotten wetter on the drive.

Nick's hands wrapped more firmly around my waist, and he raised me to the hood of the car. The engine rumbled under me softly, and Nick moved in closer.

"Let's take this off," he said, lifting my blouse over my head and deftly unclipping my bra. The clothes fell away, and he took one breast in hand and clasped his warm mouth to the other. I arched my back and a sigh went through me; I grabbed for his shoulders to keep him there.

He left my breast wet, and moved to the other, looping a strong arm around me to hold me in place.

"I like that, Nick," I said as he sucked and squeezed.

It felt good to have a man want me so badly. To want me badly enough to wait until the end of my shift and secret me away so he could have me all to himself. Flashes of heat danced through me and over my skin, and his hot breath wandered over me. Nick. My Nick tonight. I gripped his shoulders harder.

"You're gonna fuck me, too, right?" I panted. This man already had me so worked up. I'm sure I'd soaked my panties, maybe even my skirt by now. "You got me *so* wet, Nick."

"Are you ready?" He pulled back. Bare-chested in front of him I flushed deeper, but it was too dark for him to see it. He clasped my cheeks with both hands, holding me where he could look into my eyes.

I could sense his desire.

"Take me," I whispered, not breaking from his shining eyes.

He released me to drop his pants, raise my skirt, pull me in close, and push my underwear aside.

"How's this?" He asked, before plunging his hard cock deep inside me. He slid right in, my wetness making it easy. I hadn't even seen his cock, the darkness and the haste blurring. But he was inside me, and my chest was pressed to his. Reaching around me he held my ass in one strong hand and cupped the back of my head with the other. He stayed there for a long minute, letting me feel his full length, letting me feel the rumble of the Cadillac beneath us as he pinned me down.

"I like that," I managed through a groan. "Fuck, Nick."

He eased out slowly, letting me gasp for air. I clung to him. I could barely think, but when I did it was only about how naughty I was, sneaking out with a strange man in the night. I'd been warned about these things, and now I knew why: nobody wanted me to have this much fun.

When Nick's cock had left me empty he ran a hand up my thigh, gripping me where he had in the restaurant when he seduced me on my shift. I felt his finger enter me, feeling my wetness.

"You're quite the little slut," he whispered. "Don't you want more?"

Was he going to make me beg?

His hard cock stood erect mere inches from my pussy. My heart raced for a moment and a flash of anger passed across my brow. He was going to make me beg.

"Are you going to make me beg for it?" I whispered back, reaching out for his cock to stroke him. He was long, dripping wet from my pussy. "You don't want to make this little slut beg for her cock," I continued. "You don't want to know what happens."

Inside me he curved his finger. I swear he found the inside of my clit. I shuddered, warm ecstasy flooding my veins. I could see his smile widen and I gripped his cock tighter. I pulled. He stepped forward.

"Fill me up, Nick." I cooed.

He can't resist me, right? That's why we're here?

I felt the head of his throbbing cock spread me wide a half second later.

"I will definitely be filling you up tonight, Isabel." He practically growled into my ear, and as he pushed his way inside me again he spread my legs with both hands.

"Fuck!" I gasped.

"Just like that, girl," he growled. He nipped my ear, and moved to kiss me on the lips. Of course I let him.

His mouth was soft and warm.

Hours before I hadn't known this man existed, and now I let him part my lips with his tongue. This is life, I thought. This is how to live a good life. Don't hold back.

"Don't hold back," I whispered.

"I won't," he said, and returned to kissing me.

He held me there, on the hood of his Cadillac, and when he broke our kiss he pounded me. He thrust into me until I truly couldn't think, and the darkness melted away into a psychedelic rainbow. It was easy, my pussy drenching his cock and welcoming him in. Each thrust shook the car, and I cried out in the night.

"Fuck! Nick, fuck yes."

And he'd groan, and whisper "slut" into my ear to make me moan, too.

There's nothing like a thick, hard cock, I thought as his rhythm slowed. Nothing. I shivered, and I don't know if it was from the cool night breeze or the impending orgasm tidal wave, but I bucked under him, and he held me firm.

"Nick, fucking hell…"

"Small town slut," he murmured.

"Nick, I wanna cum first," I moaned. "I'll cum first you hear me."

"Then cum for me, Isabel." He gripped my waist firmly, holding me to his cock. I shuddered again: the hum of the car, the force of his body on top of mine — the darkness and his hot cock inside me. I came, grabbing tightly to his chest, holding him as the wave rolled through me, leaving me limp and panting on his muscled shoulders.

He let me stay there for a moment, before he eased his cock out of me.

"Are you ready for more?"

"Mhm," I said, looking up at him with doe eyes. He must have known.

He forced my legs wide again, pushing into me, filling me with thick heat.

"Good," he whispered. "What a good little slut. I like it when little sluts cum on my cock, Isabel."

"Mhm," was all I could manage again.

But he held me, not letting me slip into post-orgasmic haze until he'd cum. He shook the Cadillac with his powerful thrusts, the axels creaking back and forth until we came to a stop together, until he pumped me full of hot cum, and pulled his cock from my pussy to let it run down the black hood of the car.

"Fuck…" he groaned.

"You naughty man," I cooed, tapping his nose with my forefinger. Perhaps he could see me smile even in the darkness. "You naughty, naughty man… fucking your waitress."

"How could I resist?"

He pulled me in for a tight hug, my pussy still running with his cum.

"Nice paint job," I giggled.

"A little souvenir from a long time on the road," he whispered.

"Are you married?" I asked after a moment. It hadn't occurred to me to ask before – he'd caught me up in his eyes, his dark hair, his firm grip on my leg.

"I'm a businessman," he said.

TAKING
MAYA CHASE
RACHEL

Taking Rachel

Shortly after I began work in the sales department of Brooks & Weston Cosmetics and Materials, a new girl took the desk opposite mine. A low divider separated us, not enough to block the view but enough to afford some privacy on the desk. Her name was Rachel, and like she'd moved to Philadelphia after college for the job. I didn't pay her too much attention at first, being too focused on learning the ropes of the job and trying to impress my new boss, but before long I couldn't help but pause and listen when Rachel got on the phone with customers. Her voice was sweet and musical. I would put down whatever I was doing — shut my laptop for a minute, take off my headphones. That was when I began to really notice her. Her tan southern skin never seemed to lose its sunlit glow, and her dark blue smiling eyes flashed whenever she became animated. It wasn't long before I began to fantasize about her, and B&W's relaxed dress code certainly didn't help keep me from distraction.

Rachel was a runner, and three days a week she'd come into work in just a sports bra and tight yoga pants. She jogged to and from work those days, keeping her straw-gold hair back in a loose ponytail. Three days out of five I became rather unproductive, Rachel's athletic body taking me from my work. The curves of her ass and hips were hugged tightly by her yoga pants, and when she wore her thinnest pair even the camel toe between her thighs became visible. Her belly was firm, strong from daily exercise, and above, her breasts pressed at the edges of her sports bra. She would sit down in her swivel chair, putting a hand up to let out her ponytail and shaking the hair loose.

"No traffic this morning," she'd sometimes joke, smiling at our co-worker Lisa in the next desk. "Nothing like a good run to get you ready for the day's work."

Other times, she and I would trade greetings before setting in to our work, her smile and her absent clothing sending waves of heat through me. One Friday morning, when neither of us had very much at all to do, our chit chat ranged on longer.

"Busy day today, Ben?" Rachel's eyes flashed, and she adjusted her sports bra to better accommodate her ample breasts.

"Not today, just wrapping up a few small clients before lunch, really. I might take the afternoon off." I twirled a pen between my fore and middle fingers, and could feel a low flush come to my cheeks as I looked at Rachel. Her nipples pressed visibly through the fabric of her sports bra. "How was the run in today?

"Ooh!" She smiled. "That sounds like fun! A little extra weekend." She folded her hands behind her head, leaning back in her chair and sighing, still cooling down from her run. "I did a few extra miles this morning on the way in, went across the river, you know? I'm liking this city a lot, actually. You're new here, too, right?"

"Yeah, I just moved from Boston like a month ago. I honestly haven't gotten the chance to explore much, what with work and settling in."

"I get that." She twirled a strand of golden hair. "That's why I run, really. All the other time we supposedly have, it just disappears."

"You're right." I cracked a smile. "Gotta live in the moment when you can."

She laughed, agreeing with me.

"I can't say I disagree. Can't let youth just pass us by, can we?"

"No, we shouldn't." I noticed her long dark lashes, casting small lacy shadows over her cheeks as the sunlight from the window shifted. "Say, want to grab lunch in a bit? We really haven't gotten to know each other, despite sitting right across from one another—"

She wrapped the same strand of hair around her finger, pausing for a moment before responding. I could see her deep blue eyes deciding. I thought she'd wanted me to ask. I knew I wasn't too poorly made myself, a man of modest height and an athletic build. Short dark hair well kept, clean shaven — I'd been told my eyes were like prayers, soft and honest. Still, confidence waxed and waned, and I wasn't sure if I'd made the right call.

"That would be nice," she said, smiling broadly at me, the corners of her eyes crinkling. "Where do you want to go?"

"I hadn't thought that far ahead." I chuckled, smiling too. The warm blush returned to my cheeks, but I could see it in hers, too.

"How about we think of some and decide later?"

"Sounds like a plan," I said.

"It's a date," Rachel said. She ducked her head quickly, opening her laptop and logging in, momentarily avoiding eye contact, as if she believed she stepped too far. But a moment later she lifted her eyes to mine again, brow furrowed. She turned her head slightly, quizzically: "It is, isn't it? A date?"

"Absolutely," I said, confidently. I smiled, and relief returned to her face.

"Good," she said.

Bashfully, I put my head down and got to work.

Half-past noon came, and I was wrapping up my last client call. A small firm in Annapolis was trying to lower the their agreed payment on a shipment of cosmetic mineral ingredients, and the call went on longer than I expected. I watched the clock in the corner of my screen, anxious to leave the office and find a place to eat with Rachel. I had nothing to worry about, of course. When I finished the call she was still finishing with her last client, gesticulating pleasantly and sharing a laugh with whoever was on the line. Her natural friendliness with customers was already paying her dividends, and out of those of us who were new, she was the only one to take home a bonus at the end of her first month. She was impressive, and as I set my desk in order for the weekend I listened to her, excited by her animated, lively voice. She flashed me a smile and a wink, putting up a finger to signal she was almost ready.

"Well, thank you so much Mr. Freeman… Yes, it was a pleasure talking to you, too, I'll make sure that shipment is in order by the end of the day, alright?" She laughed softly. "Yes, yes. You have a great day, too. And a good weekend! … I'm sure we'll talk soon. Goodbye!" She hung up the phone and mimed exhaustion. She was more an actress than an authentic in sales, but she was brilliant at it.

"All set?" I asked.

"Oh yeah," she replied, smiling and pushing herself up from the chair. She shut her laptop and slipped a notebook into her desk. "I think that's it, then."

We took the elevator down to Market Street. The sun shone with early afternoon light and only a few clouds darted across the sky. The weather was warm, and the scent of spring in the city filled the air.

"What a nice day!" Rachel looked to me for agreement.

"Yeah, it's brilliant," I said. We walked east, toward the Delaware river. "I know a good little boulangerie this way, if that's alright."

"Ooh, that sounds delicious." We walked briskly, Rachel's hair returned to its ponytail and her breasts bouncing only slightly as we went along, the sports bra firm and effective.

"I've been there a few times since moving here," I said. "They have this spinach and black chicken sandwich that's just irresistible."

"I bet," she said. "I haven't spent much time downtown, you know. I just run the streets."

"Well, I haven't either," I said, chuckling. "This is practically the only place I'm familiar with. A few pizza shops, maybe, but that's not date material."

"Who says!" She nudged me playfully.

"I don't want to ruin my physique on a first date!" I laughed, nudging her back with my shoulder. Her skin was warm to the touch, and I could feel the blood rush to my waist.

"You could always come out and run with me, Ben," she offered. "Eat all the pizza you want." We both laughed, turning happy eyes on one another.

Coming to the river and the boulangerie we stopped. A small wooden sign hung in the glass door. *Closed.*

"Well." Rachel looked at me and smiled teasingly. "I guess it's pizza."

"I suppose it is," I said. "And I guess I'll have to take you up on that run."

"You certainly will." She tapped my chest playfully, and I instinctively tightened my muscles. "Ooh, yeah you don't want to ruin these with a slice of cheese." She giggled, and I lowered my head bashfully.

Philadelphia is flush with Italian restaurants, and we found a dive just around the corner selling pizza by the slice. She ordered two cheese, and I got the same, and we took our paper plates and small cups of water to the high bar that looked out the window to the Delaware.

"Not bad," she said, pretending to examine the pizza like a critic. "Nothing a like a good boulangerie to get you going, wouldn't you say?"

"Couldn't agree more," I said. "This baguette is lovely."

She laughed, turning to me on her stool and licking sauce from her fingers daintily. We finished off our slices slowly, taking each other in. Now that she'd approved my physique I certainly felt as though we were on more equal terms; I'm the kind of man who assumes all beautiful women are out of my league, regardless of reality.

"Thank you for lunch, Ben." We'd left the pizzeria and were now walking along Walnut Street back towards Independence Hall. "You know, it's really hard to meet people in a new city. Especially organically."

"I know, tell me about it!" I placed a hand on her back as we walked, her electric warm skin sending an excited current toward my core. "Hey, I'm glad I asked. You know I've been thinking about it since you started, but I didn't want to make things awkward. This was fun."

"I'm glad you asked, too!" She turned to me and kissed me warmly on the cheek, her soft lips leaving behind a tingling sensation and a blush. "It's not awkward. Like I said, organic. I don't like to use apps, you know? Like, what would I tell my parents if I ended up *actually* hitting it off with a guy from Tinder?"

"I know what you mean." I laughed softly, returning her kiss. "So, how about that run, I don't want to let this pizza destroy me. I know you wouldn't want me then!"

"I'll think about it," she teased. "What's your mile?"

"Fastest, or average?"

"Whichever will impress me, silly."

"Well, my fastest is just under 5:45…"

"Ooh, now that is impressive," she said. "Yes, I think I could run with you."

"Oh you could?" I laughed, teasing in return. "Well, who said I could design to run with you? What's your mile?"

"Doesn't matter," she said, smiling and whirling to tap me on the tip of my nose. "Faster than yours! Race you to the end of the block."

She was off, her powerful legs launching her forward and her golden ponytail streaming behind her. Her tan arms and athletic torso moved gracefully through the air. I followed, with nobody on the street at this time of the workday to get in our way. I watched the curves of her locomotive ass tense and release as I gained on her, meeting her at the end of the block in my work clothes despite her head start.

"Nice job, rookie." Rachel took my hand and pulled me in for a kiss, her soft lips meeting mine and our hot breath mixing after the sprint.

"Thanks," I said, pecking her back. "I live around here, actually, mind if I change into something more accommodating? I can't keep up forever in these." I indicated my salesman khakis, green button-down shirt. I looked like a Land's End advertisement — sure, to her perhaps a sexy Land's End advertisement, but no runner.

"Be my guest." Her blue eyes flashed, dark lashes fluttering. "If I can come up, that is."

"I wouldn't think of stopping you," I said. "It's just down this street."

We came to my apartment building, an old newspaper office that had been converted into studio apartments and two-bedroom units. I lived in one of the cheaper ones on a middle floor, overlooking a long

Philadelphia avenue, and on a good day receiving a fair amount of sun. I led Rachel up the steps and into the small elevator. I thanked my good sense that I'd made my bed that morning, and that I kept a decent home.

"Welcome to my home," I said, opening the door for Rachel and letting her enter first. I'd left the curtains open, and the studio was filled with bright sunlight. "It's not much, but it's comfortable."

'Oh no, it's lovely!" To our right was my little galley kitchen, and beyond that a moderate living room with a couch and loveseat, both in blue-grey. I'd dressed the floor there with a soft rug, and on the wall my bookcase stood full. To our left was my bedroom, private only by a sliding frosted-glass panel that doubled as a door for the small bathroom. "It's really quite cute." Rachel took off her shoes and flopped down on the loveseat.

"Thanks," I said.

"You change, I'll wait right here then we'll go out."

"Ok," I replied, coming up to her and offering her my mouth for a kiss. She seized the moment, our hot breath mingling. "Mmm," I murmured, putting a hand on the back of her head, lacing my fingers through her hair and tracing the length of her upper lip with my tongue. She responded in kind, nibbling at my lip and meeting my tongue with her, then pulling away.

"Go now." She winked, eyes smiling. "Don't keep me waiting."

I went to my bureau and pulled out a pair of running shorts and an athletic tee. Sliding the bedroom screen closed, I unfastened my pants and took off my green button down. My cock had stiffened in my boxers, and I could feel the strong urge to let it free. I was naked except for my underwear and socks, and after a moment's consideration I removed the socks.

"Hey, Rachel?" I called.

"Yeah? You ready?"

"Yeah, how does this look?"

Through the frosted glass I saw her stand come to the door. She paused only a moment before sliding the door open to find me bare-chested and rock hard. I spread my arms and smiled, showing off. A look of shock momentarily flashed across her brows before she spoke.

"You look…" She looked me up and down, not failing to notice my throbbing bulge, practically bursting from my fly. "Very good, Ben." Her arms were spread between the door and the frame, as if holding her up.

"Sorry if I startled you," I said, laughing softly and grinning foolishly. "I just thought, you know…"

"No," she said, putting a hand to her mouth to stop a giggle. "No I think you're hilarious, and… and hot." She stepped further into the room, closing the narrow gap between us and placing a hand on my chest. Her touch was cool, but it nevertheless sent heat radiating through my body.

"Hey, you're pretty hot yourself." I smiled and placed both my hands on her shoulders, leaning in to kiss her softly on the cheek, and then the other cheek.

"I mean…" Rachel dipped her head. "I try, you know."

"I've noticed," I said. "I couldn't help but notice you at work, since the beginning Rachel. I mean, damn, you come in wearing nothing but a sports bra some days." I pushed her lightly to the bed, into a sitting position. "Your ass, Rachel. Sometime I can even see your…"

"My pussy?" Rachel winked at him from her seat on my bed.

"Just a little." I smiled, spreading her legs apart with mine and standing close to her chest, my hands still firmly on her shoulders. I pushed her then onto her back, to the bed.

Her deep blue eyes went wide.

"What are you doing, Ben?"

"What do you think I'm going?" I slipped my fingers under the waistband of her yoga pants, rolling them slowly over her hips.

"Are you going to fuck me?"

"Yes." I yoga pants had passed her hips, and I slid them down her thighs. Rachel lifted her legs for me, making it easier to take them off completely. "Do you like this?"

"Yes," she said, smiling from below me. She'd thrown her hands above her head, and she lay there watching me proceed with undressing her. Off came her socks, then I was over her, lifting her sports bra over her head and shoulders as she raised herself slightly.

Rachel's breasts were freed, large smooth rounds standing from her chest, lush and ready to be devoured. She was mine now, and she knew it.

I helped her move further onto the bed, so her knees no longer bent over the end of the mattress. I lay between her outstretched legs, just high enough on her body so my lips could reach her breasts. Her skin was sweet and warm, the rounds of her breasts marked with goosebumps of anticipation. I ran my hand along the inside of one leg, and Rachel moaned, the cool electric sensation of my fingers no doubt turning her on. I reached her pussy, soft to my touch. She'd become wet for me, her labia dripping with desire. I wanted her, too.

"Shhh." I put a finger to her lips to stop her from making a sound as I stroked the length of her wet crease. I'd fantasized about this since I first caught a glimpse of her in snug, skin-tight pants. She clearly didn't wear underwear, wanting to be noticed, not wanting the sharp panty-line across her ass.

"Ben…" She whispered despite me, smiling and finding my eyes as I kissed her nipples gently. "Ben, don't tease me like this."

I couldn't release her breast, deciding instead to leave a dark mark on her skin above the areola on her right bosom. I kissed between her breasts, my head fitting snugly into the warmth smoothness of her bust.

"I want to tease you," I said, raising my head to meet her wide blue eyes. With two fingers I separated Rachel's labia, running my fingertips along the inside length of her wetness from her clit all the way down. She moaned, twisting under me at the sensation.

"I want you," Rachel groaned, arching her athletic back and pushing her body up at me.

"I know." I moved to her next, cradling her head in my hand and kissing from her ear to her breast, around and up again to the sensitive part below her chin. She murmured my name, moaning at my careful touch. All the while I caressed the soft skin around her pussy and traced a line from her navel to her clit, knowingly sending tickles of sensual energy rushing over her core just as they rushed through mine. My cock ached to fill her, to feel her strength clench around me, pulling me in and inviting me to cum deep inside. "Rachel?"

"Hmm?" She smiled with her eyes closed as she tried to answer me.

"Do you want me to fill you up now?"

"Mhmmm." Rachel grasped my waist and pulled me closer, drawing my body to hers so my hard bulge pressed against her pussy. She drew my head close to hers, whispering in my ear and drawing her teeth across her bottom lip seductively. "Fuck me."

I brought Rachel's hands to my boxers, allowing her to pull them past my waist and down my legs. She sat up, looking at me, biting her lip, wide eyed and waiting. Fuck I wanted to take her. I could feel the blood pumping through me, my heart racing, my cock hard and throbbing before her. She waited. I placed a hand on her chest and a finger to her lips. Pushing her back onto the bed, her loose hair falling haphazardly around her face, I knelt over her between her legs. Rachel's long tanned legs, toned and thick from running many miles each week, reached up over my shoulders. Her pussy waited, and so did she, her deep lake-blue eyes finding mine again, darting over my chest and down to my cock, and returning to me.

Placing my hand over her pussy and spreading her open I could barely hear her yelp over the pounding in my own chest. The head of my cock slid into her easily, and she tensed and arched under me, shuddering as she took me into her body. Rachel exhaled powerfully, clawing at the sheets and clenching around my hard cock. She only calmed when I was fully inside her, the tip of my cock pressed up deep in her pussy. I let her acclimate before pulling almost all the way out again.

"Ooh!" Rachel gasped as I retreated from her pussy, her eyes watering. I slammed into her again, pressing her down with my hand to prevent her from shifting while I fucked her. I kept her legs propped aloft against my chest, and I could feel her quickening pulse and the rapid tensing of her thighs as she took my length.

"Rachel," I moaned. "This is what I wanted."

"I know," she said, breathing heavily and reaching up to grasp my shoulder. I squeezed her breast softly in response, not pausing my long thrusts. She moaned and panted below me, and I thought I knew what Rachel was feeling, the electric pulse of my cock between her legs, the shiver of energy running from her thighs to her clit. With one hand she rubbed her clit softly, much slower than the pace of my thrusts, but just enough to fall into my rhythm. She closed her eyes again, no doubt in ecstasy from the double pleasure to taking cock and measured masturbation.

I ran my hand along Rachel's smooth chest. I'd wanted this for what seemed like so long. I'd seen her; I'd wanted her. Who wouldn't? I desired her with every fiber of my being, aching to fill her up. And here she was below me, legs against my chest, sighing with each thrust. The sheets crinkled around our bodies, and the bed shook with the force of our movement.

I closed my eyes, and the moment I did I felt a hand on my chest, pushing me up and away from Rachel. She brought a leg down from my shoulder, and added the force of her thigh, compelling me to pull out. I opened my eyes and looked at her. She was grinning mischievously and meeting my eyes, sitting on my bed, legs apart, pussy dripping onto my sheets.

"I want to ride you." Rachel bit her lip; she'd discovered it turned me on.

"Alright," I said, taking a moment to adjust to the loss of control. Until that moment I'd dominated her. I'd taken the confident runner girl to bed and had my way with her, did what I wanted to do. Now she reached up and took me by the shoulders, turning me and pushing me onto the bed. Rachel straddled me, her pussy rubbing up against the full length of my hard cock, still dripping from being inside her.

"Like this," Rachel said, winking. She placed a hand on my chest, and with the other she reached for my cock. The afternoon sun turned her into a golden silhouette, and a goddess as she took me, slowly. Rachel eased onto my cock, allowing the head to slide between her labia before entering her, and even then ever so slowly descending onto me. She closed her eyes and exhaled, moaning as she came to the end of my long shaft, the tip of my cock buried deep in her pussy now, making her shake.

Rachel moved her hips against me, grinding her pelvis against mine and moaning with each repetition. The movement against my cock felt sweet and heavenly, soft as she clenched around me. This was the girl I'd dreamed about, her legs spread over me, wrapping my waist. Her breasts hung above me, and I couldn't resist lifting my head to kiss each tit, her firm bust swaying into and out of my reach with her movement. She rode me hard, groaning, feeling my full length inside her. And Rachel overwhelmed me, the warm wet grip of her pussy around me drove me to the edge. She noticed as I in turn clawed at the bed, seeking to keep hold of myself.

"What? I'm going to make you cum, Ben?" She chewed her lip, leaning into me harder, working the full power of her ass to fuck me.

"Oh… yes, yes you are," I managed. Under her I was suppliant. I was at her mercy and she took full advantage of the moment, pressing into my chest for better leverage, forcing my cock ever deeper into her dripping pussy. She fucked me powerfully and rhythmically, grinding into me, moaning, tensing. Her hand had stayed on her clit, and she moved her fingers deliberately to her own motion, preparing to cum on top of me.

"You can cum when I cum," Rachel chided softly.

"Oh, my god." It was all I could manage. "Rachel, you're so fucking hot."

"I know," she whispered. "Oh, Ben! I'm almost there." I could see her abs tense, and I could feel the same pressure around my cock as she clenched her core, tightening around me, readying her orgasm. The moment came, her body shaking as she continued to press her pussy over my cock, taking me as deeply as she could. Her temperature rose, and the sun flashed through the window as she came — she tossed her golden hair and let out a long ecstatic sigh. Rachel rubbed her clit still, the vestiges of the wave crashing through her. Through her breast I could feel her heart pounding, and felt the warmth of her quick pulse.

I squeezed her breast as I came, placing my other hand on her ass and pulling her tight, forcing my aching cock as far into her as I could. I exploded: I couldn't hold back the pressure that had built in me, and I released a flood of hot cum deep inside Rachel's waiting pussy. Groaning, I pulled her tight to me.

"Yes, cum for me baby," she murmured as I moved my hips to get the most I could from the climax. The warmth spilled all around us, our bodies moist with each other's sweat and cum, the mingling scent of our sex growing in the air.

On top of me, an inch from my face, she looked down at me and smiled, her lake-blue eyes glowing, her dark lashes fluttering. Rachel was beautiful over me like that, my hard cock still pumping her full with heat, and her heart still racing with mine.

"Thank you," she said, and she kissed me. Our lips met with soft relief, the last exotic tension of our orgasms melting away into hazy bliss. We rolled over, and she pulled me tight so my cock wouldn't slip out of her wetness. Our kiss was long, and small tears or ecstasy ran from the corners of her pressed-shut eyes, landing on the bridge of my nose. I felt the heat on Rachel's breath, the energy of sex.

Slowly we untangled our bodies, coming together in kiss after long kiss — soft lips meeting and retreating, eyes finding each other and sparkling with shared rapture.

"Rachel," I said after a while, pulling from a warm kiss to look at her stunning face.

"Hm?"

"This was a good fucking afternoon." I grinned, and kissed her again, our tongues finding each other for an endless burning moment.

"It was," she said. "I'm glad you took me home."

"I'm glad I took you."

"I didn't have much of a choice, did I?" She teased, poking at my nose playfully. "What, a hot guy like you wasn't going to let me go."

"No," I said. "No I wasn't going to let you go. I need a beautiful girl like you in my life."

"And I need a man who fucks me on the first date." Rachel laughed, slipping one leg between mine. We kissed and became familiar with each other's shapes as the afternoon grew old, and as the last light of day trickled over the horizon Rachel ran her hand over the length of my body. "Second date?" she asked.

EX
MAYA CHASE

ONE

Jalen adjusted the back of his seat, returning it to
the upright position as his flight cruised low over the
Hudson. He'd boarded that morning following a flurry of
hugs and goodbyes at the end of an all-too-rapid freshman
year at UCLA. Everything had gone by so quickly: he'd
joined a music group where he learned the keyboard, and
he switched his major from politics to Spanish. He'd made
friends with dozens of interesting people, including a
computer genius from Nevada and a girl who'd grown up
with her own horses in Kentucky. He'd changed his style,
going from the stonewashed jeans and unbuttoned flannels
of high school to a more classy corduroy and black t-shirt
vibe. He'd spent late night learning Mario Kart in his dorm;
he'd been forbidden video games at home all his life and
told to focus on grades. The freedom was intoxicating. The
memory of a midnight run to IHOP after a late physics
exam flashed through his mind. Going home felt like a
relief, though, after the endless run of parties and
homework and clubs and exams and new friends. His
phone buzzed to life as they plane came into range.

—*Hey hon I hope your flight went well. See you on
the ground. Dad and I are in the parking lot text us when
you land,* his mom texted.

—*Just landing,* he shot back.

—*See you soon. Will meet you inside.*

The baggage carousel wound its way around the mottled steel column. Jalen didn't yet see his bag, a large black suitcase with a far-too-obvious UCLA tag. He'd gotten into the college merch trend, wearing a university track jacket over his dark tee. It worked, though, his updated wardrobe accenting his athletic build, and jacket giving him the comfortable approachable demeanor every college student requires. Eventually the bag appeared, and Jalen seized it, wheeling it through the swinging double doors to the arrivals area where his parents stood ready to welcome him.

"Well done, son," his father said. "One down, three to go." He was a powerfully built man, still several inches taller than Jalen. He gave him a strong pat on the back and a hug before allowing Jalen's mother to effuse her joy at seeing her boy.

"Oh Jalen, you look so handsome! I wonder if your friends will even recognize you! Look at this," she said, tugging at his jacket. "My college boy all dressed up and ready to meet the world." She gave him a kiss on the cheek and a long hug. "It's good to have you home, hon."

"Thanks, Mom, Dad," Jalen said. "Yeah it's good to be home. I mean, it'll be good to take a break, too before jumping into the summer, you know."

"Of course, baby why don't we get you to the car and we can grab some lunch or something on the way back."

"We can go to the Liberty Diner," his father chimed in with a grin. "I used to go there all the time as a kid. I must have taken you before, Jalen."

"I don't think you have, Dad," Jalen said. But a New York diner? Who could resist after months in the Golden State.

The Liberty Diner in Queens had Formica tables wrapped in chrome straight out of the 1960s. Red pleather booths, red pleather bar stools, chrome clocks, neon. Flavored syrups, a dessert card, and coffee sugars stood at the end of the table by the wall.

"Ah, nothing's changed," Jalen's dad said, chuckling and opening his menu.

"Ross you always were one for nostalgia," Jalen's mom teased. "Now what will my boys be having today?"

"Man I haven't had a legit New York bagel in forever," Jalen said.

"The things you miss," his mom said wistfully. "I remember coming back after my freshman year. Back then bagels hadn't even migrated to DC."

"I think you're lying, Mom."

"I am not!"

"She's not, son," his dad cut in, jesting. "I don't think you should question your mother's memory. She must have a lot stored up in there after all these years of gossip."

"Ross!"

"Oh it's true Betty! And you know it!"

"Well, if you must. My first summer back was too much fun Jalen. All of us got back together, the friends and all. We must have spent half the time at Coney Island. It was nicer back then, you know."

"I didn't know."

"Do you have plans with anyone yet, Jalen?" His father asked. A cute brunette waitress arrived at the table, notepad in hand. Her skin was sunny and clear, and on her round breast a nameplate read *Annie*. "Hi, I think I'll have these pancakes right here. Make sure they put some extra butter on top, I like it that way."

"Of course, and you, ma'am?"

"Not yet, Dad. I haven't really had time to make plans," Jalen said as Annie took his mother's order. She came to him. "I'll get a coffee and a bagel with lox, please."

"Of course, I'll be right back with those drinks." And she was off.

"So no plans yet, huh Jalen?"

"No, Mom. I'm sure something'll come up. I'll text Dev after this."

"What about Amy? You going to see her?" He mom narrowed her dark eyes at him across the table. "I'm sure she'd love to hear from you."

Jalen's ears went hot.

"No, I bet she would not. We've been over this, Mom. It wasn't a great breakup and I'm not about to go meddling with things right when I'm back."

"Alright, well then you'd better start looking elsewhere, a young man's not going to stay fresh forever."

"Mom!"

"Betty just let him be."

"I mean if you're not talking to Amy then you might as well get Annie's number..." she mumbled off, playing with a packet of sugar like a child.

"Who?"

"Just the waitress." She cast her eyes out the window the way mothers do when they embarrass their children by choice.

"Oh my God, Mom."

"Betty give him some time to breath for God's sake." But his dad was smiling, too.

The food arrived swiftly and Jalen found himself eyeing Annie, the waitress as she set down his plate. She was attractive. She looked sort of Colombian, bit also white. Nice, tanned legs that ran up into a pair of black working shorts. She had a nice nose, too: cute and not too sharp, complimented by mellow teal eyes. Hair kept up nicely in a ponytail. Jalen was sure his mother caught him looking. And he caught himself thinking that this girl was nothing compared to Amy. But Amy wasn't thinking about him, he told himself, so he shouldn't think about her. It was over. He forced his mind elsewhere.

Biting into a bagel again *was* a luxury of New York he'd missed. For all its sunshine and palm trees, LA couldn't really compete with this city's signature. Jalen's parents finished off their pancakes and eggs, and his mother insisted Ross leave a generous tip.

"Let's get you home now why don't we," he father said, standing up and stretching.

"It's about time! This boy looks like he's had enough parenting for the summer already," his mother joked, leading the troupe out to the luggage-laden car.

TWO

Amy Morgan was on the last chapter of *Little Women* as her train chugged into Penn Station. She was a bright student, her first year at Yale not failing her in the least as she took on both philosophy and economics. The moral of the novel didn't escape her. Still, she couldn't help long for a Laurie of her own, someone *she* could love, care for, devour. What's independence without a little spice? Even a little security? How about love? It had been months since Jalen had broken it off. She missed him. Pulling into the vast city which brought them together reignited the memories she'd put to rest and the passions she'd stored away.

It hadn't been her choice to end things. She'd tried her best.

—*Why can't you just fly out for a weekend? I want to see you, it's not the same long distance.* Jalen's texts had gotten desperate, heated even.

—*I just can't babe, I can't afford it.* Her replies didn't satisfy him. Things had gotten worse. He texted, he called. They traded pictures. Phone sex? She'd tried.

He was jealous when she posted photos with her new friends: —*Who are those guys?*

—*New friends! I want you to meet them, they're nice.* But inside she worried. He hadn't been like this in person. This possessive. Had he become insecure?

And then it broke. They saw each other at Thanksgiving. They'd slept together, briefly. It had been hurried. He'd caressed her body like he always did, stroking her legs and tickling her tummy before fucking her senseless to the sound of her moans, his cock almost too large for her tight slit and the rhythm of his thrusts driving her wild.

But then the next week he texted, out of the blue.

—I don't think we're going to work out. I'm so sorry, Amy. I don't want to hurt you by dragging this out but I've been feeling this way for a while. I'm really sorry for the way I've acted the past couple months. I know I seemed jealous. I just couldn't take the distance... His text went on, a long rambling hodgepodge of sentences strung together loosely with emotion. She was devastated.

The train ground to a halt at the same platform from which she departed that November after Thanksgiving. He'd seen her off, giving her a tight hug, an "I love you," and a long kiss on the lips before she climbed into coach and was on her way. That was then. This was now. There was no Jalen on the platform waiting for her. At that moment he was enjoying a cream cheese covered bagel in Queens.

The uptown E was virtually empty as it plunged onward through the tunnel beneath the park. Amy sat on the blue plastic seat, contemplating. She wasn't even sure if her parents would be home to greet her; they were both so busy, spending long hours at the office. James Morgan, her father, worked at a small investment house on Wall Street trading options. He liked his work. Her mother, Clare Morgan, was something of a legend in the media circuit, the former editor of the New Yorker and now CEO of a medium-sized online media company with dozens of websites. Amy didn't see much of either of them.

—Almost home, she texted in her family chat, lugging her big suitcase up the stairs at the 103rd St. station. No immediate response; both were too busy, it seemed, to take note of their daughter's arrival. Her father finally responded as she rounded the corner to her building, the briny smoky scent of the familiar city refreshing her, making her feel at home.

—Changed the code. 1929 now. Good to have you home sweetie.

—Thanks Dad see you soon, she typed back.

The apartment was smaller than she remembered. It always was. The spring semester had gone by quickly, but she'd grown accustomed to the open sweep of Yale's green campus, the large halls and wide common areas. Amy's childhood home was by no means spare. It was comfortable, well-kept, and well-decorated. All her memories hid here, some in open defiance, the family photos hanging on the wall, and some waiting to be seen, the little trinkets and gifts Jalen had given her through their years together, forgotten in drawers and boxes and nooks and niches in her bedroom. Setting her suitcase gratefully on the floor Amy exhaled, surveying the little room she'd grown up in.

She'd been home at Christmas, but this felt different. She'd changed in that year, and the old quilt, the One Direction posters, the dog eared copies of Dickens all felt smaller and a little bit distant, like the objects in a still life graced by the rays of a never-fading afternoon sun. She would acclimate, but she felt a little like a giantess in her own home, the muscle memory of light switches and which doors needed a little extra tug not quite coming back to her yet. Her phone buzzed: Mom.

—Dad and I'll be home early tonight. We're taking you out to Sofia's! Reservation at 8, love you xoxo see you soon. Sofia's was for special occasions. It was fancy even by their standards: small plates, moderate portions. Delicately prepared vegetable and thinly sliced meats braised in who knows what delicious spices. And their lasagna wasn't your average brick, either.

—See you soon, just unpacking.

Putting her clothes and books away in their places Amy stumbled upon a note Jalen had left sometime during their senior year. It was at the bottom of her underwear drawer, where she often little secret things hidden so her mother wouldn't find them. The note had been taped to a set of marvelously soft lingerie she'd worn for their first time. She'd kept it, even when they broke up; it was a relic too precious to throw away even as he left her. "I think you'll need these for after our date tonight," it said.

Amy had put them on carefully, letting the fabric tickle her soft skin, slide into place over the subtle mount of her pussy, and cup her full breasts like gentle black clouds. She'd been more than excited. Jalen had taken her to a little French restaurant on the other side of the park, and after giddily eating very little they'd rushed back here, to her bedroom, where her dark God had spirited a bottle of fine wine. It had been slow; he'd kissed her everywhere, fire dancing across her skin as the wine moved her stomach and her man moved her soul.

He'd smiled, he'd kissed her, he'd run his hands over every part of her waiting body before he'd asked, "Are you ready?" and she'd nodded.

The soft length of his cock went on forever, pushing into her like nothing ever had before. She'd clutched the edge of the bed and closed her eyes and moaned in shock and ecstasy. He'd soothed her through the pain, pausing and letting her gasp for air, the muscles in her sopping pussy throbbing and wanting more. And when they finished her kissed her gently on the forehead, stroking her body in rhythm with the gentle waves lapping through her core. They'd looked into each other's eyes and knew they'd lost track of time.

The memory blended with the quick love they shared over Thanksgiving, their last. The two were nothing alike, the first magical and filling a whole year's time in Amy's mind, the last a flash of brightness which flickered out in a moment.

Tears trickled from the corners of her soft blue eyes. Amy put the card back in the drawer, heaping her underwear on top of it, hiding it, pushing the memories away. It had taken her months to get over Jalen, but the pain seemed fresher at home, as if it were new again. It would pass, she told herself.

At Sofia's soft Italian music played. Dimmed sconces illuminated a long room with small black tables lining the right hand wall. It was a small restaurant, but classy all the same. Waiters in black jackets and neat little aprons tipped large bottles of dark wine into patrons' waiting classes and delivered white plates on which sat legs and pastas and ornately cut vegetables treated with a variety of artistic drizzles. The Morgans sat at a table near the front of the restaurant, a bottle of wine between them and warm smiles on their faces.

"I know you like this place, and I thought it would be a nice treat for you coming home," Amy's mother was saying. "I think they came under new ownership this spring but I don't think the menu changed a bit. Ooh this ravioli sounds delicious. Prosciutto, truffles…"

"So how's this Henry guy treating you," Amy's dad asked as her mother drifted away on different pasta fantasies.

"Oh, I broke up with him a while ago, Dad."

"I didn't know that, sorry."

"No I didn't tell you, it's fine. He was pushy and honestly I just wanted to focus on my studies, and I joined this comedy group which took some time…"

"You don't have to explain yourself, honey. A lot of people have a brief relationship after a long one's ended, but it's not often that it works out. Your mother and I have both been there, haven't we, dear?

Amy's mother was miles away in the soups. A Tuscan bisque, a fish stew from the south.

"Oh yeah," her mother said.

"See," Amy's father continued. "We've all been there. Besides that, then. How's this comedy thing?"

"It's going pretty great, actually. I got to do part of a set at a campus bar place at the end of the semester."

"That's great! I'm really proud of you, Amy."

"Thanks Dad, that means a lot."

The family ordered food aplenty. More hard rolls with soft insides; the finest olive oil sprinkled with salt mined in the Italian Alps; imported bass; a cheese board; the truffle and prosciutto ravioli Amy's mother had been eyeing. The wine flowed. The questions were endless: Amy, tell us about these new friends of yours; Amy, do tell us about these professors; Amy, have you thought about what you want to do this summer.

"So, Amy," her mother said, carefully dividing a ravioli with her fork. "Have you made plans with friends yet? I heard something from Ellie's mother about a party going on, are you going to that?"

"I haven't heard of any party yet, but I'm sure I'll see people soon. Like I said I'm just going to settle in, look for a job or something. I don't really no. I haven't really gotten in touch with anyone yet."

"You're probably going to run into Jalen at one of these things, hon, have you thought about that? I don't want you caught off guard," her mother went on.

"I hadn't thought about it," Amy lied. She had. She didn't know what she'd say. He'd liked pictures she posted with Henry, the briefest of college boyfriends. Would he ask about him? Would he be jealous? Would the whole thing be awkward?

"Well, I'm sure it won't be that bad. Just be civil," she continued. "I know things didn't end well but do take the higher road."

"Don't worry mom," she laughed.

"Ok, well I've said my piece," she replied, smiling at her daughter. She took another bite of the ravioli and let out an audible yum. "You've got to try this, James."

"Don't mind if I do," he said, taking a pocket of the pasta on his fork. It was delicious; everything was. It was difficult to go wrong at Sofia's.

The Morgans talked away the evening in that cozy dining room. Patrons filled their bellies and wait staff flitted back and forth between tables, querying their satisfaction, collecting glasses, pouring drinks, processing payments, smiling, delivering ever more dinner rolls. Amy was glad to be home, and glad her parents had taken the time to book a meal for her return. When the door swung behind them and ushered them onto the warm evening street the sun was just setting, the long summer day just coming to an end. The clamor and heat of New York that had been quieted by the comforting walls of Sofia's rushed to greet them, and as streetlights flickered to life and lamplight drifted from apartment windows into the darkening city night Amy and her parents walked home, happy to be together again. For the moment, any anxiety Amy had felt about Jalen was put to rest.

THREE

Jalen tried to wrestle the controller from his younger brother, Herb. They were playing Grand Theft Auto in Herb's room, chatting away the afternoon and downing bags of barbeque flavored potato chips.

"Look at this," Herb said, pointing to a building in the game. "Like, is that real?"

"I think it is, it looks familiar."

Herb had been asking pretty much the same question all afternoon. Since the game's map was based on Los Angeles, he stopped his stolen car every few blocks to point out one conspicuous building or another and ask Jalen if he'd seen it. He'd stopped in front of the big Oriental cinema, a Chinese-gabled building on the boulevard. Jalen looked it up: yes, it was based on a real place. Now could he please have a go, they'd been road tripping instead of actually playing the game for far too long now.

"Cool, and how about that one."

"It's a fucking gas station, Herb. I don't know," an exasperated Jalen laughed, remembering why he loved and hated spending time with his brother. "Now gimme that."

"Just one more, I wanna see how you've been living in LA."

"Not like this bro," he chuckled to himself, taking another handful of the chips.

"Fine, then what's it like. Do you fuck bitches?"

"Jesus, Herb."

"What?"

"Not really the language I'd use," Jalen said. "Girls aren't bitches. Is that what you guys say at school?"

"Whatever, man, you know what I mean. You been laying pipe?"

"Ok, fine," Jalen gave up, not wanting to fight him on it. Let the parents handle it. "I'm doing fine with the ladies but I think I'll keep that to myself."

"Then I bet you haven't been having much luck. Sorry, bro," Herb needled. "Better luck next year I guess."

"It's not that bad," Jalen said, folding. "I've had a few here and there. I'm just not going to discuss my sex life with my brother, now can you hand that over?" He took the controller. And it really hadn't been bad. He'd met girls at parties, through mutual friends, and one classmate of his, Amber, had even come up behind him to tap his shoulder after class. A little banter, and the two of them had skipped classes for the rest of the day, legs intertwined and laughing smiled spread across their faces as they shook the dorm room twin bed. Besides Amy, Amber had been the only girl he'd fucked who could take the full length of his cock. It was hard to cum when a girl could only take the first several inches, but Amber was incredible. She'd turned onto her belly and lifted her ass for him, begging he pound her as hard as he could. And oh boy he did: she wailed and bit hard on her pillow, her pussy dripping wet to accommodate his deep thrusts. She'd shuddered when he came inside her, the pressure unbearable. He was the first man to make her cum just by plowing her, she'd told him. They'd cuddled and kissed and had a few more sloppy rounds of sex: she'd ridden him, crying out with no pillow to bite on, and he'd held her legs against his chest as she lay on her back taking his long dark length fully into her body. So no, no he would not be discussing his sex with Herb, eager as he may be to know the secrets college girls kept.

The cars zipped past, the dull colors of the game flashing by as Jalen sped along the loop road. He crashed, his character's body flying through the windshield and crumpling like a paper doll against the grille of an oncoming truck. He handed the controller back. He'd never had the touch for this; furthermore, he was annoyed that his parents had folded so easily to Herb's demands for a console when he'd gone without one all through high school. Oh well. Herb took them back toward downtown Los Santos, cruising up to the Vinewood sign and stopping the car.

"So, Jalen, if you're not gonna tell me about California girls, then you'd better tell me whether this sign exists in real life."

"Not like that it doesn't. Fuck off and give me the controller back, Herb. Don't be annoying." The two brothers continued, falling back into the rhythm siblings have. It was good to be home, Jalen acknowledged, even if he had to put up with this.

As the evening approached and he waited for his mother to call for dinner Jalen lay on his bed. The blue duvet of his youth was worn, but comforting, bringing with it shards of memories throughout childhood and adolescence. Dark nights of youth when his mother read him a bedtime story and turned off the light as she left the room. Warmer nights, high school nights, when he lay here with Amy and she let him touch her breasts for the first time. She'd wanted him to: "I know I'll like it. Don't be nervous," she'd giggled. Now he flipped through Tinder. All sorts of girls flickered before his eyes: demure book types, edgy artist girls in turtlenecks, girls flaunting their large breasts, girls with cats, athletic girls who could outrun him in any event, girls with dogs. Jalen unconsciously compared each and every one to Amy. Somewhere in the back of his mind he regretted calling it off. He knew she'd gotten together with another guy pretty soon afterwards. Maybe she was happier with him. He was pretty sure his name was Henry. And sure, he'd slept with a few other girls himself. Amber. But he'd compared her to Amy, even then, in the midst of what sex any other freshman boy would kill for. Soon Jalen realized what he was doing, and the comparison became conscious. He put the phone down after a while; he couldn't bring himself to swipe on any of them.

Just as his mother called him to dinner Jalen's phone buzzed. He'd left it lying by his head, worn out from looking through girls he couldn't want. It was Dev, his best friend from high school.

—*Hey man, I'm throwing a party Saturday at my place. It would be great if you could come. The whole gang's gonna be there and we can all catch up. Lmk asap I'm buying drinks later.*

FOUR

True to her word Amy tried her best to search for a summer job. She would rather die than work retail, and she'd rather suffer the humiliation of taking a temporary position under either her mother or father's offices than work in food service, but she hoped to find something professional, yet not too demanding, for the length of the summer. It was a difficult screen. Nobody wants college freshmen, and beyond that nobody wants college freshman for a semiprofessional role. She clicked on a link for a file clerk at a downtown law firm Kutchensen Howard & Belson. Scrolling through the page she looked the like of the job. They firm handled mostly intellectual property law, not that it mattered when you were filing documents. Amy clicked on the button to apply, and uploader her skimpy resume.

Back on the main page after submitting her application she let the cover reel run, reading more about the firm. Ideally she would have done this before applying, but it couldn't hurt now. A man's face she recognized popped up in the slideshow: *Ross Howard, founding partner. Ross has been with KH&B since its founding in 1996. He earned his undergraduate degree in psychology at CUNY and went on to…*

"Shit." Amy closed her laptop and flopped backward on the bed. She'd just dropped her resume to Jalen's dad's law firm. He wouldn't see it, though, she comforted herself. Surely some receptionist or lower level clerk would scan her resume and reject it out of hand: another unqualified freshman looking for easy money. The gears spun in her head as she fretted, anxiously blowing the problem up in her mind, bigger and bigger with each turn of her brain, like a balloon ready to burst. Questions. Jalen. Worries. Jalen. Job. Jalen. Jalen. Jalen.

Amy heard the front door open and the quick clomp of her mother's shoes being kicked from her feet.

"Amy?" She called out.

Amy brought herself back to earth. Everything would be fine. She'd find more jobs to apply to later. Plus, she should have some fun for the rest of the day anyway.

"In here, Mom."

"Been up to much today, hon?" Her mother's voice approached. She came to the doorway, leaning on the frame and surveying her daughter's room. Amy's suitcase lay open and empty in the middle of the floor, and Amy lay on the bed looking up at the ceiling.

"Not much really just looking for jobs."

"Yeah?"

"Yeah."

"You don't look so great is something wrong?"

"Nah nothing's wrong. Just tired." Amy sat up, propping herself up on her elbows and shaking the worry from her face.

"Well, tell me when you're ready if it doesn't just blow over."

"Oh, mom." Amy laughed. She couldn't hide anything from her mother.

"I'm home early, want to do something?" She asked, changing the subject. "Come on, let's go get some takeout for when your dad get back."

New York in May is much nicer than New York in June, but it was already getting hot that time of year. The sun was high in the sky, the longest days of the year rapidly approaching and 5:30 becoming a second noon.

"Let's go across the park," Amy's mother suggested, putting a hand on her daughter's shoulder and giving a gentle nudge. "You still look glum, Amy, what's eating you?"

"It's not much Mom, just embarrassing." They crossed onto the grassy tree-lined paths of Central Park. "I just accidentally applied for a job at Jalen's dad's law firm."

"Accidentally? Isn't Howard in the name?"

"Yeah, it is."

"Amy, Amy, Amy," her mother laughed, shaking her head. "I'm sure it won't matter."

"I hope not," Amy laughed, too, the anxiety dissipating.

Across the park they came to one of the billion Chinese take-out restaurants in Manhattan and ordered a few of the various combo meals drenched in truly American sauce. Nothing Chinese about it at all, but they didn't mind.

"Maybe Jalen could get you that job, Amy," her mom ribbed. "I think he owes you one anyway."

"Mom! He does not. I haven't talked to him in months."

"Oh sweetie I'm just kidding. Can you hold this my phone's vibrating." She handed over the paper bag and answered. A business call.

Looking about the park as they walked Amy took in the sycamore trees, their spotted grey bark like camouflage. People jogged over the footbridges and sat on benches looking out on the ball fields. This whole city had been hers and Jalen's. No, she would let sleeping dogs lie, no matter how much she missed him. And she acknowledged that she did. Maybe she could have fought harder to keep him: called him up, pleaded. No, she would have seemed desperate. He was an ex, now, nothing more. She would go home, have dinner with her parents, and text her friends. Maybe she'd even meet a cute boy on a night out; you never know.

Back on her block Amy handed the paper bag back to her mother to check her own phone which had buzzed in her pocket. There was a party going on the next day, a text read. Be there, or be square.

FIVE

The bass thumped loud. People had gathered in the several rooms of Dev's Madison Ave apartment and the drink was flowing. Dev had gotten the good stuff, dark beer from upstate and imported red wine and scotch. He surely intended to throw the finest party of the summer and set it off on the right foot. Friends from high school and Dev's pals from NYU mingled, and before long the chairs and sofas in the main living room had been shoved aside to clear a dance floor where young bodies moved and gyrated against each other like it was the roaring twenties again. And if anyone were to be our Gatsby, Dev was the man.

"Got a drink, man?" Dev threw an arm around Jalen. They'd been best friends all through high school, and while they hadn't talked much that year, the excitement of their new environs distracting both, the bromance had not vanished.

"Yeah, I've been sippin' all night, Dev, this is great. Fucking amazing party, bro."

"Thanks, means a lot," Dev shot back. "Maybe you can pick up a new girl tonight. I only just heard about you and Amy earlier. You shoulda told me, man." He gestured to the dancefloor with his free hand, the one that held a long-stemmed glass of wine. "Anyway, there's plenty of opportunity out there Jalen."

"I know," Jalen said. He smiled at his friend. "I'll see what I can do. Tell me about NYU, though, you said you wanted to catch up."

"Yeah, man it's been a lot. Honestly it was a hard year for me," Dev started. "But hey, let's sit down if we're gonna do this."

The two friends made their way through the mass of people to the kitchen. Others fluttered through to grab drinks, but Jalen and Dev took stools in the corner and nobody interrupted. Jalen poured them both fresh cups of wine.

"So go on," he said.

"Yeah," Dev looked away. "I'm just not sure I was ready for the pressure, you know? I spent a lot of time partying," he gestured to his guests. "Not like this, but you know. Still."

"I get it," Jalen wrapped his hands around his cup, resting them on his things pensively. "It was a lot to get used to for me, too. Sorry I wasn't in touch much, even the little time zone thing threw me. I mean I was busy trying to get my rocks off after breaking it off with Amy." He took a drink. "And that didn't go too well."

"Awe, sorry man. Women are tricky."

"Yeah no shit—"

Their conversation was interrupted by the opening of the door to the apartment. People had been coming and going all evening, but at the sight of Amy in the doorway Jalen froze. She was beautiful; more beautiful than he remembered, wearing a thing silver chain around her neck that drifted dangerously close to her plump breasts. She wore a low cut black top and an incredibly short red skirt. He could see all of her. The outline of her hips which he used to hold tightly as she rode him. Her nipples through her braless outfit. Her hair was done up in a loose bun, and her eyes flashed over him, too.

She saw a man she'd lost. His muscular arms and soft brown skin drawing her in with memory and regret. He hadn't grown less attractive in their time apart; if anything he was more a man than when they'd parted. He'd grown slightly, and between his long powerful legs her eyes found the contours of his bulge.

"Um, Dev..." Jalen stammered, whispering, suddenly at a loss for words. "I didn't know Amy was coming."

"I mean, we're friends, man,"

"Yeah—"

"Hey, Jalen," Amy cut in, walking around the kitchen island to the men after taking off her light jacket. "It's been a while."

"Um, yeah, hi" he said, still finding his tongue. "You look really nice, Amy"

"Thanks," she said, pulling at the edges of her skirt out of habit. The compliment really did flatter her. Sure, it was awkward, but it wasn't as bad as it could have been. "You do, too."

"Hi Amy," Dev said, welcoming her with a hug. And to Jalen: "I'm gonna check on the rest of the party."

Jalen's eyes pleaded with Dev not to leave him standing there with Amy, but Dev didn't bite. He stepped away, leaving the two looking awkwardly at each other by the cluster of bottles at the side of his kitchen island.

"So," Jalen said.

"Yeah," Amy replied, awkwardly. "Um, how's California?"

"It's pretty good. Warm. Can't complain."

"Yeah?"

"Yeah. Do you have a new boyfriend, Amy?" Perhaps his voice came out sharper than it should have. She flinched.

"What, you jealous all of a sudden?" She asked defensively. Amy reached for a red cup and poured herself an ample shot of whisky.

"No, um, I'm sorry. I was just asking."

"It's fine," Amy replied, downing the drink. "We broke up."

"Oh, I'm sorry."

"You?"

"Yeah."

"Ok." And a moment later. "Ok, sorry I didn't mean to be aggressive."

"It's fine, neither did I," Jalen said. The two had gotten that surface tension out of their system. *Dance Monkey* thumped and rose and fell in the background, almost overshadowed by the loud murmur of the partygoers. "Want a seat, Amy?"

"You mean sit here and talk with my ex instead of going in and, like, dancing?"

"I guess."

There was a long pause between them. Amy took a sip of her new drink. The air was clouded with differing emotions. Jalen could smell Amy's perfume, a mix of the sea breeze and the flowers of an open meadow.

"I mean, sure." She sat on the stool Dev had vacated, facing him. "So, Jalen, what do you want to say to your ex?" She sipped her drink, meeting his eyes. In that moment she didn't know what she felt. She'd loved Jalen so much. He'd broken her heart. He seemed so vulnerable here.

"I don't know, Amy." Jalen sat there, moving his cup to his lips but not drinking. "I mean, I'm really sorry about how we left things. I shouldn't have broken things off like that."

"You mean that?" Amy struggled to keep the tears in check. He pulled at her heartstrings.

"Yeah," he lowered his head. "It was really shitty of me to just text you out of the blue. Look, we all make mistakes, and I'm not trying to justify mine but I'm saying it was a mistake, I should have—" He didn't complete his thought. He couldn't. Jalen didn't know where he was going with it. Should have what? Shouldn't have broken things off at all? Or should have waited and said it in person? Or should have called? Amy noticed his furrowed brow and extended a hand, placing it gently on his forearm.

"It's ok," she said. "You hurt me a lot, Jalen, but I understand. I know we talked about it, but I don't think you ever saw how hard it was for me, too—the distance."

"No, I did." He said, meeting her eyes again, not brushing off her touch. This conversation was long overdue. If it were a library book, he thought, he would owe his savings.

"You did?"

"Yeah, and I just wasn't empathetic enough, I guess. I've grown a lot, Amy. I've learned a lot since we dated."

"Me, too," she said.

"Sorry," Jalen began to apologize again. "I know this is overdue. Do you think we can go on with a clean slate, Amy? Be friends?"

"I'd like that. You've always been my friend, Jalen. Before… even while we were together you weren't just my boyfriend you were my friend, too. I think it's possible."

"Good," he said. "Good, good." And he took another swallow of wine. He felt the electricity between Amy and him that had always kept them going coming back to life. Should he say something? The wine said yes, his reason said no. "Want to go into the main room, there? It's a bit drafty in here." It wasn't drafty at all, in fact, and he didn't know why he'd said it.

"Sure," Amy said, finally withdrawing her hand, self-conscious that she'd left it there so long. She got up and filled a third drink.

The two took a seat side by side on one of the couches that had been pushed to the edge of the dancefloor. In front of them bodies moved together in desire, one young man pulling the woman he danced with close against his hips and swaying carefully into her to the tune of *Senorita*. They kissed, and touched foreheads, the man's hand straying to her ass and squeezing seductively. Amy felt her cheeks flush with the help of drink, and Jalen didn't fail to notice.

"Dev sure throws a hell of a party," Jalen said, drawing Amy's attention from the couple she'd fixated on. "I mean I don't know half of these people."

"Me neither," she replied, laughing, knocking her knee into his accidentally at first, then leaving it there to see if he'd notice. Of course he did. Was she flirting with him? Surely she knew they didn't have to go through the motions all over again. But she continued: "And I think most of these people must be his friends from college. I mean I don't even *recognize* them, let alone know them. Oh, wait, there's Jane. And Michael. Ok so a few friendly faces…"

Amy began counting off their mutual friends and acquaintances, finding faces in the crowd of dimly lit students and pointing them out to Jalen.

"Yeah," he joined in. "And there's Harry and Eric over there."

"Eric?"

"You knew him, didn't you?"

"I don't think so…"

"He was kind of nerdy in school, you know," Jalen said. "He looks different now, I think he got a haircut. Thank God."

"I really don't think I know him, Jalen."

"He had big hair!" And Jalen mimed an afro. "I think he goes to Penn now."

"Oh, maybe I knew him in passing," Amy conceded, giggling at his hair mime. It was these little things she missed about him most. The things she couldn't replace with Henry. She looked around for someone he might not know, and finding one: "Ah, over there we have Jasmine, in the red dress. Cute, isn't she."

She was right. Jalen didn't recognize her, and now in her little game of find a friend she'd set a trap. She didn't have to; she could have been up front. She felt the chemistry, too. Of course she did: it wasn't she who broke it off in the first place.

"I mean, I don't recognize her," Jalen said, sidestepping. Then, taking the bait: "And ok sure she's cute, but not as good looking as a certain girl I know."

He smiled at her. A clean slate, he'd said. You can flirt with a friend, right?

"And who would that be?" Amy set her cup down on an end table and edged closer to Jalen. "Who's this mystery girl who's more attractive by far than Jasmine in the red dress?"

Amy's breasts were too near to Jalen's face. Some things naturally make a man's blood run hot, and one of those things is a pair of breasts he's spent nights nuzzled against, kissing softly, leaving little purple marks against the soft pink skin.

Jalen's tipsy eyes fell slightly, from Amy's kind features to her breasts, and then back up to her soft eyes. This was the girl he dumped? Fuck. *She* didn't deserve that, a kind and albeit dashing woman like her. He'd already had several drinks, and it took Jalen's mind a moment to realize all this thinking was taking pause. He had to answer her.

"It's you," he said matter-of-factly. "I mean, look at you. Fucking gorgeous even at Dev's dance party."

She was taken aback, not ready for him to come out and say it. Amy had been counting on luring him out slowly; and she hadn't even decided how far she would go. Did she want him back? Or did she want to make him realize why he wanted her back, and remain just out of reach? All she said was "Thank you," lowering her eyes to her cup to process.

"Amy, I didn't mean, um—"

Jalen would hang himself on his own words.

"You don't mean it?" She lifted her doe eyes.

"No, I mean, yes—Um, I didn't mean to come onto you like that, it's not right, but—"

"Keep going," she coaxed. Men: it always takes them a long time to get their words together, she thought.

"I mean, you're very pretty, especially tonight. Definitely prettier than that girl—"

"Jasmine."

"Prettier than Jasmine, yeah, but like I know it's not right to flirt with you, 'cus, like I broke up with you, and all."

She was half enjoying him muddle through his thoughts, the wooly hair on his scalp flowing back and forth as he wrinkled and unwrinkled his brow. He'd set his drink down and was moving his hand around in his lap as if gesticulating would help the words come out cleaner.

"Jalen," Amy said, putting a stop to it. He stopped, looking at her.

"Yeah, sorry I sort of lost my train of thought there."

"No shit," she giggled. "But, hey…"

"What?"

"I think you're kinda cute, too."

"Oh yeah," he said, breaking into a huge grin, the anxiousness draining from his deep well-meaning eyes.

"Yeah," Amy said, "I do." She couldn't hold his gaze, the flush burning in her cheeks. Was she proud of this? What would come of it? What *could* come of it?

"Amy, can I tell you something," Jalen ventured after another pause. The tune had changed and the dancers on the floor moved quickly up and down, pulsing their fists and belting out the lyrics. Jalen didn't hear it, caught in a slower universe.

"Sure," she said, still not meeting his eyes.

"I," but he fumbled immediately. Catching himself with a breath: "I regret breaking up with you, Amy. I really do. I wish I hadn't done it."

Now she looked up, a mixture of fear and relief and wonder stretching across her cheeks as she blossomed.

Eyes smiling in the dimness Amy couldn't help but lean in closer to the man in front of her.

"Do you really mean it?" She asked, catching herself and giggling. "And don't stammer your way through a minefield for me just say yes or no."

"Yes," he said, and leaned in for a kiss. Amy did, too. Their lips met, heads tilted slightly. It was a kiss they'd built up to, and a kiss they had missed. Jalen placed a hand on the back of Amy's head, gently biting at her upper lip, tracing the rim of her mouth with his tongue. She replied with a tug to his bottom lip and a little moan, which she quickly silenced. Pulling apart they looked into each other's eyes in search of an answer to the one question: Was this true? Amy found her answer.

"I think I needed that, Jalen," she said.

"Me, too," he responded.

"What do you say we take a walk," Amy said, standing and offering her hand. They left the music behind and returned to the kitchen, tossing their emptied cups. Jalen helped Amy put on her jacket and then he searched for his shoes.

"They always had incredible chemistry," Dev noted to Jasmine as Jalen and Amy headed out the door. He silently forgave Jalen for not saying goodbye.

SIX

Jalen and Amy walked south on Madison Avenue, hand in hand. Their fingers were laced together tightly, and in the dimness of the city night they held close to one another. As soon as they left the party the words seemed to vanish between them; neither knew particularly what to say. Each thought their own thoughts, the maelstrom of emotions and confusion turning their stomachs about. At a crosswalk at 59th Street the silence finally broke between them. The two had walked nearly ten blocks.

"I'm really happy, right now," Amy said, turning to face Jalen as they waited for the light. No cars approached, but they took the chance to pause and look into each other's faces. "Thank you. Really. I've missed you so much, Jalen you don't even know."

"I've missed you, too, Amy," he replied, caressing her rosy cheek. "Can I be honest?"

"Of course," she said, smiling. "That's all I ask."

"I've been comparing every girl I meet to you these past months."

"Oh my god, you have?" She laughed, her eyes crinkling in the corners, delicately. "That's so cute and funny."

"It is?"

"I've been doing the same thing. I'll be honest, too, that's why it didn't work with Henry."

"The boy you were seeing?"

A green man appeared in the little black box and the two young people crossed West 59th and continued southward on Madison.

"Yeah, he was kind of annoying," Amy said.

"I know what you mean," Jalen chuckled, squeezing her hand harder. "Tell me more, though about how he compared to me. I want to know everything."

"Jalen! That's a bit nosy don't you think, prying into your ex's love life!"

"Perhaps," he said, smiling.

"You have to tell me how other girls live up to me, first," she said, teasing him. "I haven't seen any new girlfriend online, so I suppose none of them could," Amy continued.

Jalen reddened and suppressed a chuckle.

"I mean, you're not wrong," he said. "None of them could live up to you."

"Ooh, pray tell," she whispered. "I suppose nobody could kiss as well as I can?"

"No," he said, "they could not."

"Well, you're not exactly spilling secrets here Jalen but I guess I can tell you that Henry's lips weren't nearly as soft as yours. And he didn't keep himself clean shaven so his stubble tickling my legs wasn't very fun."

"Your legs!"

"Well, a girl's got to have fun," she chided.

"So does a man," he said. "But I can tell you there's nothing more disappointing than not getting yourself all the way inside a girl." He flushed, looking down at the black spots of gum on the sidewalk. Had he advanced too quickly? No, she squeezed his hand tightly.

"I bet," she said, and she kissed him on the cheek. "I won't pretend I don't know how good I am for you," she went on. "All those nights, Jalen…"

"I know." He squeezed back and met her eyes. There was the sheen of little tears in them. Jalen had missed her terribly, he knew it as the feeling formalized deep in his soul. Not just her body, but her kindness, her understanding, and her wit.

It was late when the two of them reached Battery Park and found a solitary bench to overlook the midnight harbor. Lady Liberty stood as a grey silhouette against the glow of New Jersey and Staten Island. The face of the

Colgate clock shone from across the river. In the darkness Jalen pulled Amy close, wrapping his arm around her as she lay her head with its soft long hair on his firm shoulder. The fire had been rekindled between them, and both wondered why they'd ever left the hearth in the first place.

"This is nice, Amy," Jalen said. "I guess this is what it feels like to start over."

"I suppose," she said, leaning into him further. "I like it. I'm glad you're here."

"Not exactly a clean slate, though," he laughed. "I know too much about you, gorgeous."

"I know," she said. "But it sort of helps to know what you're getting into."

"Yeah," Jalen replied, and they looked out over the water in silence for a while, hands interlinked and bodies nestled together on the bench.

"You want to know something funny?" Amy asked after a while, finding Jalen's eyes in the darkness.

"What?"

"I accidentally applied for a job at your dad's firm yesterday. I was really worked up about it for like the whole afternoon. He probably won't even notice—"

Jalen laughed, his dark eyes smiling.

"No, he actually mentioned it," Jalen replied, unable to wipe the grin from his face. "He asked me about it at dinner and I was like 'I dunno.'"

"Oh my God," Amy said, flushing in humor and embarrassment.

"I know," he continued. "We were all kinda wondering what was up with that."

"I swear it was an accident," she giggled, clutching his arm.

"I'm sure it was," he said. Their eyes met and Jalen placed a hand on Amy's shoulder to bring her in for another kiss. Their warm lips met, an oasis in the cool May night. In the distance horns honked, but for the moment the only world the was the one of contact between man and woman. Amy's warm breath tickled Jalen's clean-shaven chin as she nibbled on his lip, and in turn his tongue outlined the soft interior of her upper lip. She tasted good; the trace flavor of whisky and wine on her breath, wine on his. There was, too, that illusive taste that only comes with desire: the warm electric almost mythical taste of a lover.

Jalen pressed a hand to the fabric over Amy's firm breast, and a soft moan caught in her throat. She'd missed this. She'd missed him. She could feel the strength in his hands as he held her, and she felt the heat well up in her core saying *more*.

"Maybe we should call and Uber," Amy said softly, breaking the kiss, pecking him lightly again on the lips. "This is a park bench, after all."

"Sure," Jalen said, pulling out his phone but going in for another kiss, feeling the dewy warmth of Amy's perfect lips against his. "Ok," he said. "Your place or mine?"

"Well," she teased, tapping his nose with her forefinger. "I do have the larger bed..."

"Yours it is, then," he said, smiling and pulling her close. "I've missed you, Amy."

"I've missed you, too, Jalen," she said.

Jalen kissed her neck softly as they waited, the smooth surface of her skin bringing back every memory, every moment when he'd laid her down below him, her hair scattered about her head, every moment he'd climbed over her and kissed her gently around the collar, down around her breasts. *This* he'd missed.

The car came, a little black thing with T&LC plates.

"For Jalen?" The driver asked.

"Yes," he replied, helping Amy into the seat first. "Thanks, I know it's late..."

"No problem at all! We're going to 103rd I see? Shouldn't take long at all at this hour."

And it was late. Past midnight by this point. They'd walked for a long time, and sat for longer, because as everyone knows time passes differently between lovers, especially at night.

The car cruised uptown, and in the back seat Jalen and Amy held hands tightly.

SEVEN

"My parents are probably asleep," Amy said, punching in the code and unlocking the door to her apartment. "Be careful."

"Don't worry," Jalen said, putting a gentle hand on her waist.

Amy led him down the hall to her bedroom where light glowed from under the door, a lamp carelessly left on before the party. Opening the door, she pulled him inside and the fell on each other ravenously. In a moment's time their bodies were pressed together, and Jalen held Amy in a tight embrace as he kissed her, their lips opening, tongues exploring each other's warmth, eyes closed as energy danced across their skin.

"Amy," he whispered, pulling from the kiss and tucking his face carefully against her ear, holding them there for a long moment. "Amy you're the sweetest girl I know."

"And you, Jalen…" she intoned. "You're a good man and I want you back."

"Me, too," he said. "I want you, too."

Amy carefully unbuttoned the dark blue shirt Jalen had one, exposing the soft fuzz and toned dark muscle of his chest. She kissed his chest, working her way toward his navel as the buttons came undone. At his belt she stopped, looking up at him for permission. He nodded, stroking her soft hair and releasing it from the messy bun.

She unclasped the buckle on his belt, sliding the leather out and freeing the button of his corduroys. They were soft pants; she liked this new style. Pulling at Jalen's waist she lowered the pants to his knees and, turning him, pushed him to sit on the bed. She ran her hand over his stiffening bulge, the contours of his firm cock fully visible through his black briefs. Amy had missed *this* penis. Henry had been smaller, fucking her hard until she cried, yes, but ejaculating far too soon, and she'd never cum just from the feeling of his cock deep inside her. With Jalen it had been a regular occurrence.

Taking the elastic waistband in both hands Amy rolled the briefs down, pulling Jalen's underwear and corduroys off around his ankles, leaving his long legs bare. His legs were thickly muscled, and blossoming from between his thighs his massive dark cock stood erect, a full vein pulsing, the skin around his balls tight with anticipation. Leaving the clothes on the floor at the foot of the bed Amy moved to take his thick shaft in her mouth; the soft throbbing head felt warm against her soft lips, and at the touch Jalen let out a low groan. Wrapping a small white hand around the base of his cock Amy held firm and stroked his thickness in sync with the motion of her mouth. She emitted little gulping sounds as she sucked, tasting his sweetness; manly musk rolled from him and filled her nostrils, and she sighed inwardly with bliss.

Amy tried her best to maintain eye contact with her man as she devoured his long cock, the silky tip basing again and again over the roof of her mouth and down her throat, almost choking her. Each and every time she felt the full length of Jalen in her mouth little tingles coursed over her skin. While she sucked on his cock Jalen grasped her hair, moaning at the warmth and wetness working on his shaft.

Jalen's body was running hot, his muscles tense as he sat on the end of Amy's bed. He still worse his blue button down which hung loosely around his shoulders, but everything else had fallen away, his lean dark body firm and attractive in the lamplight. Amy had placed a hand over his abs to feel him tense and release as she swallowed his cock, sloppily devouring his length and massaging his shaft. With one strong arm Jalen held himself up in a sitting position; the other he'd dedicated to Amy's luscious hair, strands of silk between his fingers.

Before long Amy's mouth grew tired from holding Jalen's hefty package, and she withdrew, tracing the length with her tongue and leaving a long trail of kisses right up to the tip, where in a moment of passion she lapped up the precum that flowed there. Her touch on the most sensitive point of his body sent electric chills coursing through Jalen's strong body, and he moaned again, sighing and breathing heavily when she finished. Blood pumped through his cock with such vigor that it stood as hard as ever, dripping and ready to be engulfed in a woman's tight core.

"Come here, babe," Jalen said, raising both his hands to the height of Amy's breasts and tugging at her top. "Why don't you take this off."

She raised her arms and allowed him to lift the shirt from her chest, rolling over her head and off her arms until she stood before him topless, glowing.

"Like what you see?" She teased.

"Oh, I do," Jalen replied, leaning forward and pulling her in to access her breasts. He nuzzled her first, feeling the soft warm skin and the round buttons of her nipples brush over his smooth cheeks. The feeling was electric; it brought back the hundreds of times they'd done this before. The ecstasy; the love; the endless passion day in and day out for years. He kissed her firm breasts, lovingly running his tongue over her areolae and suckling lightly. With a firm right hand he held her back and with the left he gripped her right breast, the other he greedily consumed, tickling her with his teeth and caressing her with his warm lips. Amy sighed as he did, and the faint scent of alcohol mixed with her fine perfume wafted to his nose, buffeted by a wave of musk and loving heat that poured from both of them.

"Jalen," she moaned. "Please, take me."

Picking Amy up Jalen set her on her bed. With a strong grip he pulled her skirt and undergarments free and she bent her legs in compliance. He shed the loose shirt and they were both naked on her quilt, dark God over glowing light. Before fucking her Jalen leaned in to kiss her pussy. It was warm and waiting and wet, and she smelled sweet. He tasted her, and warm ecstatic memories filled his mind. On his knees before his shining girl Jalen dove in, his lips becoming wet with her sex; with his strong hands he spread her legs as far as he could, feeling the softness of her inner thighs beneath his fingertips. She tasted sweet and earthy, and her strong scent lured him closer. She moaned and twitched as his tongue flitted in and out of her drenched pussy, over her labia and to her clit. She yelped, crying out and moving a hand to her own mouth to keep silent as he made circles over her clit, her little button sending electric waves through her core with each pass of Jalen's warm rough tongue.

"Fucking take me, Jalen," she moaned. "Fuck…"

But he didn't let up, placing a careful hand on her belly and pressing softly as he ate her out, lapping at the wet opening of her vagina and coaxing even more sighs and moans from the rosy girl before him. With a free hand Amy held her breast, squeezing it with anticipation, her whole body tensing under Jalen's methodical caress. He wanted to make her cum just like this, give this to her as penance for his ignorance, but just as she was near climax, shuddering, the muscles in her core hot and tense, Amy pushed his head back and looked him in the eye.

"Jalen," she whispered, moaning. "I said fuck me."

Jalen nodded, crawling forward on his knees until his cock barely drifted over Amy's aching pussy. He ran the head of his powerful cock between her labia, accumulating her wetness, stroking his cock with the moisture to lubricate it. She wanted him more than she ever had; it was as if it was their first time all over again. Amy shivered in anticipation, her breasts tremoring.

Goosebumps lined her arms and chest and her wide eyes met his.

"Baby," he said in a gravelly whisper. "Oh, Amy."

Jalen aligned his cock with Amy's pussy, resting the head at her hot opening and in each strong hand taking one of her ankles and spreading her legs wide and back over her. He slid into her slowly, his thickness parting her tensed muscles. She yelped, her eyes watering as she stifled a shriek by bringing a corner of the quilt to her mouth. She melted under him, the muscles in her core giving way and going slack. She flushed, waves of heat coursing across her skin and through her chest, breasts heaving.

"Amy," Jalen moaned, sighing in his own right, the wet warmth enveloping his cock almost more than he could handle. She took him fully, the crest of her pussy pressed firmly against his balls, against the pulsating base of his long cock. He could feel every inch of her around every inch of him, the walls of her pussy hugging his thick shaft and welcoming him home.

In a moment he was pounding her hard, adjusted now to the feel of her moisture, her powerful heat wrapping him up. Jalen held her firmly in place, plowing his full, thick cock into her and pulling almost all the way out. She yelped every time he plunged back in, shuddering. Hot tears escaped from her pressed-shut eyes as she took him, all of him. This was not just now, it was every time before relived and brought back. The feeling of a man's rigid thickness parting her like fire was truly more than Amy could stand, the power of his thrusts, the constant movement of this strong thighs pushing his cock into her again and again — it drover her wild.

Amy's abs tensed, the cool flame of desire rushing through her and stopping time. Even before she could open her eyes she was cumming, shaking as Jalen's unrelenting energy thrust her over the edge of an invisible cliff, pushing her to climax. She bit hard on her quilt, grasping for Jalen with one hand while the other clawed at the sheets. Heat sprang from every pore, her skin was aflame and she was a star ready to burst. She let the quilt go to let out a long sigh—

"Oh my gosh, Jalen, you fucking God. Oh boy…" she heaved, the electricity still coursing through her body in warm spasms. "Kiss me, oh my god. Don't stop…"

He didn't stop, but he slowed to a gentle pattern, sliding his pulsing cock in and out of her gently as she recovered. Their lips met in ecstasy, the thrill of the soft tingling between their mouths a welcome change from the recent flurry of movement. Jalen kissed the corners of Amy's mouth, the angle of her lips soft and smiling beneath his. He bit at her neck, leaving a dark heart-shaped mark on her left side and returning to her mouth for another long, hot kiss.

Jalen and Amy lay together, feeling the warmth radiating from each other's bodies. They kissed and nuzzled and felt each other's bodies, reminding themselves of the familiar contours, blemishes, and features of the other's form. Jalen's cock remained stiff and ready, pressed against Amy's soft throbbing pussy. She ached from being spread so wide, from taking Jalen's thickness in her core. But she wanted more, and she wanted to finished him off.

"Are you ready for me, Jalen," Amy whispered after a while, her hot breath warming his ear. He was; he nodded and met her eyes, lifting his head slightly to kiss her lips as she rose over him. Kneeling, she straddled him, his dark body below him like hills at night, and she was the goddess of the moon. "I'm going to fuck you until you cum in my pussy, my beautiful boy," she said, pinching his cheek softly as she positioned herself. Her breasts swayed as she adjusted her body, transfixing an all-too-ready Jalen. Amy's hair fell like moonbeams down her back and around her remarkable face.

Gripping Jalen's still pulsing cock below her Amy lowered herself onto him, throwing her neck back instinctually and letting out a long sigh as he filled her. He moaned as she engulfed him, her warmth flowing over him. Adapting again to the thickness between her legs, filling her up deep into her core, Amy began to move her hips. She knelt with her legs spread wife, her thighs wrapping Jalen's waist, and she could feel all of him yearning beneath her.

She tensed and releaser her strong ass muscles and begged him to meet her with soft thrusts. Moaning, gripping his waist, and gyrating her wide and gorgeous hips she rode him. Jalen held her, too, grasping her around the middle and raising his head to kiss her breasts as she worked her pussy hard against his middle. His full hot length was buried in her wetness, pressing into her core, wrapped tightly in her pulsing muscular pussy. It was a soft and consistent sensation to have her body moving back and forth over him. She forced little thrusts of his cock by moving her hips just so, the resulting moment of pressure almost enough to shove Jalen over the edge, too.

Amy moaned and exhaled loudly as she lifted herself up, only to plunge Jalen's cock back inside her. The angle was just right for the soft head of his cock to rub against her g-spot as she moved thus, and she rose again to retrace the sensation. Jalen felt it, too: the surge of energy that build from the tip of his cock as it rushed past the soft ridges of Amy's vaginal walls. It was a hot rush, made more intense by the slapping sound of their wet midsections, Amy's cum dampening their skin. The pressure built in the place behind Jalen's cock, throbbing through his balls. He let out a soft groan and his thighs tensed as he let out a torrent of hot cum, the liquid surging into Amy's wanting body. She felt the flood inside her and moaned; she'd missed the feeling of this man's enormous cock sunk deep in her pussy, releasing his the full force of his climax inside her. Jalen moaned again and pressed Amy's hips to his with the full strength of his arms, the space between them now nonexistent.

"Just like that, baby," he sighed, the tail end of the wave crashing through him. And he let got, the strength momentarily gone from his strapping form. His cum trickled from Amy's pussy, down the shaft of his cock, collecting at the base and dripping onto the bedclothes.

"Oh my God, Jalen," she whispered. "It's been a while, baby."

"It has," he whispered back, exhaling and closing his eyes. "You felt too good, Amy."

"Oh no," she giggled. "You did. I can't believe it, I just can't…"

She collapsed over him and they held each other in a long embrace, the warmth of their bodies soothing each to sleep. It was early morning now, the rosy dawn just beginning to run her fingers along the horizon. Amy snuggled close to Jalen's chest, his cock still snug in her pussy. He pulled lifted his body slightly with some effort and pulled the sheets around them. Wrapping his arms again around her smooth body he slept; she'd already begun to nod off on his chest.

EIGHT

Light was streaming through the high windows of Amy's room when they two lovers awoke. The clock on her bedside table read just past noon. Amy had fallen from Jalen's chest in the night, but lay curled into him now, her morning vision still fuzzy with sleep as she search for his eyes. They met, and then their lips met in a kiss, the traces of sex and evening still on their breath.

"Good morning, love," Jalen's said, breaking into a wide smile.

"Good morning," she replied, running a cool hand over his chest and finding his cock. "We had fun last night, didn't we?"

"Oh, I believe we did," he said

"It's good to have you back, Jalen."

"You, too, Amy. I'm sorry I ever left. I won't ever again."

"You mean that?" She asked, tears glistening in her bright eyes.

"I mean it."

"I love you, Jalen," Amy said. Parting his soft lips with hers.

"I love you, too," he replied when the kiss broke, and he pulled her close.

"I've always loved you," she whispered into his chest, hot little tears falling onto his smooth brown skin. "I never stopped loving you, Jalen."

"I never stopped loving you, either," he replied, tearing up himself. "I just made a mistake. It's all mended now."

Amy wept softly on his chest, loving him deeply with all her being and her soul. The feeling of the night before had not left her body, and she felt him still, the movement deep in her core as he filled her up, the flood, the wave of electricity which shocked her body every time. Jalen held her tight as she wept into the early afternoon.

When they finally got up and dressed it was almost three. Amy secreted Jalen to the shower and cleaned him off in the hot water, caressing his body and making him soft as well as smooth. They radiated like Gods when they left the apartment, wandering toward the park in the summer light, hand in hand, fingers woven together in bliss.

The rest of the summer they passed together, in love and reunited. Sex just got better, and Amy learned to take the full weight of Jalen's thrusts for longer than she imagined she could. He loved the taste of her pussy as much as he loved her gentle laugh. That first evening wore on and they walked and talked, laughing and kissing and holding each other tightly as the sun traversed its golden arc across the sky towards twilight.

Forbidden.
MAYA CHASE

THE VIRGINIA CLUB

On my eighteenth birthday my father took me to the country club and resort where he's been a long-time member. The Virginia Club was an adults-only retreat destination for the mid-Atlantic's wealthy and powerful, and since no children are allowed I'd never been able to visit. The resort is built upon Rougemont, named for the flaming fall leaves, the estate of the long-dead revolutionary hero Henderson Redstone, and the great columned mansion that sits atop the oak-wooded hill became the Main House of the Club. Our black car wound its way up the long road to the Main House, and the excitement burned in my chest. For years my father had talked about the place: all the business he'd done and all the money he'd made for our family. He regaled me yet again now as we pulled up to the high gates and a guard came to inspect our documents.

"Emia," he said, leaving one hand on the steering wheel as we pulled through the gate. "I've made a lot of money here. This club has been very good to our family, and I want you to remember it's a privilege that you're here at all. Have fun while you're here — play tennis, explore the grounds, swim, eat, you know — but I do not want you making a fool of me for bringing you here."

"I know, dad," I said, laughing away his worries. "I'll behave."

We pulled into a parking spot in front of the large oak doors of the Main House. He turned off the engine and looked over to me.

"And just one more thing, okay? If I have to take care of business, have a meeting or something, I don't want you butting in. There's plenty of stuff for you to do, alright?"

"Okay, dad," I said, unbuckling my seatbelt and opening the door.

"Happy birthday, Emia," he said.

"Thanks, dad."

The view from the porch of the Main House was breathtaking. The Virginia countryside swept out before us, green and dotted with small towns. In the distance I could make out the Blueridge Mountains, where the sun was setting. My dad put a hand on my shoulder:.

"Nice view, isn't it?" he asked.

"Yeah."

"Well, let's head inside, I called ahead for a table. You'll really like the food, Emia. Everything's cooked to perfection."

Inside the Main House we walked across the marble-floored atrium to the restaurant in the east wing of the building. It was dim, and white tablecloths hung over round wooden tables, each awith by red-cushioned dark wood chairs. Little lamps glowed from the center of each table, and the several waiters wandered in black ties checking in on patrons.

"Ah! Mr. Larkin, it's good to see you again. The head waiter greeted my father, leading us to a small table across the room. Turning a glance to me, friendly: "And who is this?"

"This is my daughter, Emia," he replied.

"Well, very lovely to meet you, Miss Larkin," the waiter said. He pulled out my chair, allowing me to sit comfortably. "Is this your first time to the Virginia Club?"

"Yes," I said. "It's my birthday, and my dad wanted to show me around."

"Very well then! Happy birthday, Miss Larkin. I trust you'll enjoy tonight's meal, and ask for me if you need anything. My name is Barrie."

"Thank you, Barrie," My father said, folding his napkin over his lap. "I appreciate your hospitality."

Barrie left us, and I turned my attention briefly to the room. It had high ceilings, all painted with scenes of love and war. Revolutionary artillerymen fired upon British ships in one arched panel, and in another a young man made love to a nymph in the forest, her mouth agape with pleasure and her legs wrapped around his waist. Equally mature scenes graced other panels, and I gasped as I noticed one where two nude men seemed to argue over an anxious girl between them.

"It's funny, isn't it?" My father asked, following my eye. "They say Redstone was a bit of a lecherous old man, but you know you just can't take down old masterpieces."

"Oh my god, dad," I laughed awkwardly, looking down into my lap. "Life was probably just war and women to him?"

"Probably," he laughed, too. "Part of the reason they don't allow kids here, I imagine."

"Probably," I mimicked.

A new waiter approached our table then. He carried two small bowls of elegant squash soup, and placed them before us.

"Sir, miss, enjoy a fresh acorn squash puree," he said. He bowed slightly before walking away, leaving us.

I took a spoonful.

"This is delicious," I said.

"I told you," my father said, dark eyes glinting proudly. "Chef Andre Michel is, I believe, the greatest cook on this coast."

"Hey, what about mom?" I asked.

"Well, now that you mention it, I don't suppose anyone can hold a candle to her," he said, breaking into a smile.

The night was young, and the dining room was still largely empty. As it began to fill, I couldn't help but notice a tall man with an elegant jawline and piercing blue eyes talking to Barrie at the door. He removed his long black coat, handing it to the waiter who stowed it before leading the man to a small table on the opposite side of the room. He was trimly built, and his hair was well groomed and dark. The man sported a closely-cut beard, which only made him more attractive, and I watched him take a seat. He caught my eye for a moment, and flashed a smile before turning his attention back to Barrie, who took his order. My father again followed my gaze.

"Who's that?" I asked, aware I'd been caught staring.

"Don't go *near* that man," my father said, his voice low and surprisingly stern.

"Dad?" I was instantly skeptical. His furrowed brows and lack of a real answer startled me. "Why?"

"That's Henry Shroud," he replied, regaining a little bit of his composure.

"And, who's Henry Shroud, dad?" I pressed.

"Okay, Emia, all you have to know is to stay away from him." He seemed anxious, as if simply being in the same room as Shroud bothered him.

I waited, staring him down with raised brows, daring him not to answer me. After too long a moment he broke.

"He runs Darkwall." My father's voice remained hushed. "He's tried to put Red Key out of business too many times, Emia. We're at war."

"See," I smiled. "Didn't hurt to explain yourself, did it?" I was bothered that it took him such effort to be honest. And it was too bad, I thought, that this Shroud character and my father were such enemies. Shroud was hot by any measure.

More patrons arrived, and the low hum of conversation soon filled the hall, the clink of glass on glass occasionally breaking the murmur. Shroud left my mind, and I was distracted by conversation and the opulent birthday feast my father had ordered. Over a juicy steak and crispy polenta I observed the faces. My father smiled and waved at many of them, and several men — all titans of one industry or another — stopped by our table to green him.

I recognized a face.

"Oh, my god!" I exclaimed, my fork clanging to my plate. "It's Clare Blackwood!"

"Your roommate?" My father asked, turning in his chair to search the faces. "I didn't know her family came here."

Clare and I had graduated together last spring at Kingstown Academy in Pennsylvania. She had filled out since I'd seen her last, her lively dirty-blonde hair pulled neatly into a ponytail that fell over her shoulder. She looked stunning in a bright yellow dress, andher blue eyes shone. I waved to her.

"Omigod! Emia!" Clare was by my side in a moment, her dress flowing gracefully around her knees as she darted to our table. "I can't believe you're here! How are you!"

We hugged, exchanging greetings rapidly. She was a year older than me though we'd been in the same class. I told her why I was here, and explained why we hadn't run into each other before.

"Well, happy birthday, Emia! We should do something tomorrow. I'll show you around, all the best spots!"

"I'd love that," I said. I was glad I wouldn't have to explore on my own while my father dealt with business. "There's tennis, I hear?"

"Yeah, just down the hill," she said. "Let's play in the morning after breakfast, they give you rackets and everything so you don't need to bring anything."

"Text me?

"I will."

She was off, sitting at a large table in the middle of the dining room with her parents. They laughed and sipped red wine, and I returned to my father. We finished off my birthday dinner with raspberry cheesecake, and retired from the dining room to my family's suite. It's always best to have a friend around, I thought.

It had rained overnight, and there was still a film of dew over the land when Clare and I reached the tennis courts. The tennis house was unlocked, and we found rackets and a ball inside. Courtside, I spun my racket and the serve went to Clare.

"I've gotten a lot better at tennis here," Clare said, tossing the ball as we took our places. "They have lessons you can sign up for, too, with real professionals."

"Oh yeah?" I bent my knees just so to ready myself for her serve.

"Yeah, last summer I took lessons every Sunday." She smiled mischievously. "That's why I'm going to kick your ass, Emia." Her serve was hard and fast, hitting the court's rubbery surface and bouncing out of reach.

"I guess it's Love-15," I said, tossing the ball back to Clare across the net.

"Get ready," she called, adjusting the racket in her hand, toying with me. The serve arced over the net, bounced once, and made contact with the center of my racket, sailing back over the net and landing just out of Clare's reach. Luck. I won the point.

"We're square now," I said, laughing. "Sorry I got lucky."

"You won't next time." Clare paced the court. She'd been my roommate for all four of my years at Kingstown. Her family is old money, and mine is new — at first she scoffed at me, superior. Over the years we grew close, though. Senior year we happily shared the podium as valedictorians. Matched as we were in intellect, I'd never taken a game of tennis from Clare. "Ready?"

"I am." I bounced the ball on the court, for luck, to center my mind. Tossing the ball in the air I brought the racket upon it like a thunderclap, sending it speeding over the net to the court surface beyond. Too fast. Too hard. It went foul, bouncing off into a mud puddle where Clare picked it up and shook it off.

"Nice one." She winked and strutted back to serving position. "Better luck next time. 30-15, Emia."

Like the first her serve was fast and close over the net. I lunged backward, stretching out my arm and returning a slow lob. The yellow ball bounced easily into her swing, and came careening back toward me before I had recovered. Somehow I made contact, and returned the ball with a powerful down stroke, right onto the court in front of Clare. Mud spun from the ball, and on the bounce it made solid contact with her breast, too fast for her to adjust.

"Ow!"

"Oh my god, I'm sorry Clare!" I dropped my racket and ran to the net.

"Emia you hit my boob! You bitch!" She looked at me with a momentary flash of betrayal. Then: "I'm sorry, I didn't mean it—"

"No, no it's fine. I'm sure it hurt. I'm sorry — I didn't mean to. Are you ok?"

"I'll be fine," she said. Then she laughed. "But you ruined my sports bra."

"Sorry," I giggled. There was a large brown spot on her right boob, the muddy imprint of the tennis ball.

"I'll just take it off." Clare reached for the elastic under her breasts and pulled.

"You're serious? What if someone sees?"

"We were roommates, Emia. Plus, it's a private club," she said, laughing. "Nobody's around, all the men are either playing golf or drinking." Her athletic body and chest fully were exposed. Yes, she had filled out, even since graduation.

I couldn't help but think she was probably right. My father was either taking shots of fancy rum with his industry friends or playing the links as a young man did all the heavy lifting for him. Ah, men.

"Up to you, girlfriend," I said, laughing too. "So, where were we?"

"It's a let," she said. She clutched her breast where I'd hit her, feigning agony. "Because you crushed my tit and it hurt like hell. I serve."

We both laughed at that, and she bounced the ball on the court before serving a quick volley over the net. She won the first game easily, and the next. I got used to her playing with her top off, though I don't think I could ever do it myself. At first I kept casting glances about with anxiety I wasn't the topless girl, but this is exactly what my father would consider embarrassing.

In our third game Clare served with a powerful stroke, her whole body moving gracefully with the swing. The ball passed me, skipping over to the courtside fence. I turned to retrieve it, and stopped short. I flushed. What would my father say? Henry Shroud stood, leaning with his elbows on the black fence, watching us play. He was wearing black aviator sunglasses and a classy blue striped shirt.

"Hey, you're the Larkin girl," he said. He took off his shades.

"Hi," I said. I peeked over my shoulder; no, Clare had not covered up, instead standing there, hands on hips, waiting for me to return to the game. Of course I knew he was here for her. Probably stopped on his way to the golf course or the bathhouse, saw a stunning topless girl and couldn't resist. They say your boobs bounce more in tennis than in track, so it's no wonder men like watching.

"So?"

It took me a moment to grasp his line—

"Yes, I'm Emia Larkin. It's nice to meet you, Mr. Shroud."

"Call me Henry." His voice was cool and soft. "Who's your friend?"

"Have you been watching?" I asked.

"Yes. You're a good duo. She looks like a Blackwood to me. A lot like Carmine."

"That's Clare," I said.

"Tell her I say hello, will you?" He asked, returning his sunglasses to their perch.

"Sure," I said, slowly. I was still drawn by his good looks, but he was drawn to Clare, barely seeing me. "You work with my father, don't you?"

He removed his aviators again, looking me up and down as if for the first time.

"Mr. Larkin and I have some business together," he said. After a pregnant pause: "I wouldn't say we work together, though. We don't often end up on the same side of the table."

"Ah," I said, drawing on words to say next. "Darkwall?"

"I'm not a friend of yours, Larkin." Shroud put the glasses back on, ending my line of questioning. The conversation was over, but the game was not. His disinterest only drew me in.

"Get over here," Clare called. "It's 30-Love, Emia."

"Showoff," I said under my breath.

We played out the rest of the match under Shroud's eye. I'm not sure his glance ever settled on me as we danced across the court, swinging and volleying and serving and laughing. Two girls, having all the fun in the world, just as we had in high school, a friendly rivalry. To my dismay he only had eyes for one of us.

We were in the Blackwood suite. Their money had helped build this club, and their suite extended for most of the top of the west wing of the Main House, overlooking the golf course, bathhouse, tennis courts, and woodlands on one side and the sloping valley on the other. The décor was old fashioned, with great oak paneling and oil portraits, red and blue Arabian rugs, ornate chairs and tables and chaise longues.

"You played well," Clare said, smirking and picking up a clementine from a blue Iberian bowl between us. "Sorry I had to trounce you."

"You always do, but you were showing off, weren't you?"

"To whom?" Clare contorted her face into a muse of disappointment at my accusation, and feigned offense.

"Shroud," I said, meeting her eyes earnestly. "He was watching you the whole time, I mean good God Clare! He was just staring at your boobs the whole time!"

"He *was* not," she intoned, peeling back the skin of her fruit. "You jealous?"

"No." But I felt the heat run to my cheeks, and she saw. I looked down.

"You are!"

"I'm not, Clare, I promise!"

"Don't worry, Emia, I don't like Shroud very much. I don't even think he's hot."

"You don't? Really?" I must have looked too skeptical. She burst out laughing, throwing flecks of clementine peel at my chest in amusement.

"Of course I do! Oh my gosh you fell for it, you did. Of course I think he's hot, everyone does. He's tall, fuck — he must get his hair cut every day. No, now I just know *you* think he's hot, and that *you're* jealous."

"I'm really not jealous." I didn't convince her.

"Emia," Clare said, putting her hand on my knee and speaking softly. "Shroud is all yours, really, I have my run of this place already. Every man in this building wants a piece of this." She waved her hand abssently toward her torso, still holding the clementine. "Really, he's yours." She leaned back. I laughed. She was serious?

"Clare," I said. "Ok, I'll admit I'm jealous. I don't have the guts to play tennis with my boobs in the open air like that. I'm jealous of that, of you. Your confidence."

"Sure," she said, slyly.

"Not Shroud."

"Sure." She peeled away a segment of the clementine and took a bite.

"Okay," I said, consigning.

"Hm?"

"Okay, I'm jealous he was paying all that attention to you."

"Ha! I knew it." Clare swung her legs down to the floor, turning her head quickly to look at me, almost conspiratorially. She spoke in a whisper. "But seriously, Emia, if you think he's hot you should go for him. You're attractive, I can't imagine he'd disagree."

"Oh my god, Clare I can't."

"But you can." She leaned in closer, her eyes flashing. "I have. With plenty of different guys. It's all about confidence. That's what you're jealous of, right? Confidence?"

"Come off it!"

"Hey, you're the one wishing Henry Shroud would look at your tits."

"Was not."

"Look." She leaned in again. "Let's just say for a moment you were confident enough to admit it. You want to get with Henry Shroud. How would you do it?"

"Really Clare, my dad told me not to talk to him. They're, like, enemies."

"Ooh, so now Shroud's even more mysterious. Your hot forbidden millionaire."

"Stop it!" Sure, I pleaded, but secretly I was enjoying it. What if…

"Let's just say, you wanted to disobey him and go after this bad boy, Emia." She smiled like a thief and popped another section of her clementine between her lips.

"Alright, let's say—"

"Let's say I dared you to fuck him."

"Clare!"

She only grinned.

"Would you?" she asked.

"I—"

"Hm?"

"Okay, I would."

"Jeez! Now it's out in the open. Damn, Emia." She waved an arm in false exasperation. We'd been here before, in high school, when Clare had spent an hour wheedling my feelings for Larry Sommers from me. She'd been successful, and even set us up on a semi-blind date. He didn't work out. "Okay now we can get down to business, sexy."

Clare scooted closer to me on the ornate couch, placing a hand conspiratorially on my thigh. She smiled, her eyes bright.

"Do you think he'll want me?" I asked, surprising myself. My lust was in the open now, I supposed.

"Of course he will!" She whispered eagerly, leaning in close. "Now, listen carefully. In the bathhouse there's a maintenance door between the men's and women's locker rooms."

We hatched a plan, involving just a little bit of seduction. The rest relied on luck — would he have me or not? He would, Clare promised: we look so much alike, she said, except for our hair. Athletic, smooth skin, long legs. Either of us would be any and every man's dream, she said.

"Okay, I'll do it," I said, my heart pounding. Heat coursed to my cheeks, and I couldn't hold back an excited smile. "I'll follow him in."

"Good." She wrapped an arm around my shoulder and pulled my ear to her lips. Whispering: "Remember: confidence, girl. You can do this. Four o'clock" She'd seen Shroud go to the bathhouse many days at four, relaxing in the steam room and hot tubs and saunas after a day of elite schmoozing or golf. He kept himself looking good, she said. Abs like a movie star, arms like Zac Efron, she said. "Go," she said. "Tell me what happens."

"I will," I said, standing up. "Thanks Clare, I needed that talk. You know how to get me out there."

As I turned to go she slapped my ass gently, teasing me. "For good luck," she said.

In my own room I puzzled over what to wear. Okay, so I didn't want to come across as slutty, even though I *was* going in there to try to fuck Henry Shroud. What further complicated things was just what exactly you're supposed to wear to the bathhouse. "Nothing," Clare had said, smirking. "It's a bathhouse." But I wasn't going to be in the nude when I met him. I was to come upon him before he'd left the locker room. I was to be discreet, luring him away to somewhere private before anyone else saw me. Between my legs I could feel my underwear getting damp. My nervousness was turning me on, and my body at least was getting ready as I fretted about what to put on.

I considered just a loose tee shirt and a pair of running shorts. That's enough to wear *to* the bathhouse, right? Nobody would suspect. No underwear, even: make it extra sexy for when he takes them off. Surprise him. Yes, I do wish I'd had the confidence to go shirtless, too, at tennis. Show off, gutsy and sexy for the CEO of Darkwall, mysterious behind his sunglasses. Who exactly would he have been watching then?

Finally, I settled on a black tank top and tight shorts. I wore my underwear anyway, leaving the bra behind. No, I didn't want it to *look* like I'd thought this through. I wanted him to sigh at my breasts, but not find my pussy too easily. Just that extra strip of cloth would keep me from being a slut, I promised myself.

The bathhouse was a large, low building positioned in the grove between the tennis courts and the golf course. Inside, it was built in the Turkish style, with columns and arches keeping the roof over bubbling hot tubs and cool blue pools. In the center of the building stood saunas and steam rooms, showers and locker rooms. It was here I went now, at just about four o'clock.

Henry Shroud entered the bathhouse before me, the glass double doors sealing behind him with a hiss. He didn't notice me as I slipped in, darting to the women's locker room. There were several other women there, in various stages of undress, chatting and laughing and toweling themselves off from their spa. They didn't pay me any attention as I coasted through the steam to the back of the room, finding the secret door right where Clare had said it was.

With my hand gripping the cool handle I paused. Was this the right thing to do? My father had forbidden me from speaking to Shroud. He'd said they were enemies in business. Was Darkwall out to destroy my family? He must be wrong, I thought, thinking about the depth of Shroud's fiery eyes. His strong arms casually propped on the fence. He couldn't be older than thirty, building Darkwall up in only five years as he did. Shroud looked good. I wanted a piece of him. I knew when he looked at me again he would like what he saw. Yes, this was the right thing. My heart pounded with excitement, and my cheeks flushed. Warmth surged between my legs and I almost lost my balance as my thighs shuddered. I turned the handle, and opened the door.

The men's locker room was the mirror image of the women's. I didn't see Shroud anywhere among the rows of metal lockers or on the benches by the showers. A few other men stood around, and I pressed myself against the end of a row of lockers, not wanting to be seen.

I heard his voice coming from around the corner. Shroud was speaking with another man about business, trying to put off the conversation until later and get on with his spa day.

"I appreciate it, Michael, really, I do, but I also just need to relax for the moment, alright?" The other man acquiesced, and I heard Shroud remove his shirt. "I'll find you at dinner, and we'll talk then, good?" They parted ways, this Michael leaving Shroud there alone between the rows of lockers. I felt like I was in high school again, sneaking around for the pleasure of boys. I peeped out from my hiding place, and seeing no one but Shroud I stepped out. His back was to me.

I walked up to him. His broad back was bare, firm and rippling with muscle. I wanted to reach out and run my hand over his sculpted shoulders, down his strong dorsals. But I didn't.

"Hey, Henry," I started softly, in a sweet whisper. He whirled around, surprised but not alarmed. He recognized me, but didn't place me immediately. For my father's nemesis he was surprisingly ignorant of me, I thought.

"Larkin girl," he said, his eyes flashing bright and his smile spreading. I was drawn to the rugged masculinity that defined his jaw. "What are you doing here?"

Now was the time to be bold, I told myself. Out with it. Honesty. Seduction.

"I'm here for you," I said, twisting my hips, just so, like I've seen in movies.

"Me? Now I would have thought your father warned you about me," he murmured, coming close, accepting my challenge.

"He did," I said, looking up at him as he approached. His chest was as sculpted as his back, powerful biceps blending into strong pecs down to brawny abs. "But you couldn't take your eyes off Clare, and I got jealous."

"Of her?" He said, chuckling softly. "I don't know why you would be." He cupped my chin in his hand, meeting my eyes. I felt wanted, in a natural, carnal way. I knew he would never love me, and I didn't want him to. I wanted this moment. "Who can resist a topless girl, especially with her confidence. But it seems you're even bolder than she is."

"Do you want me?" I asked, placing my hand in the center of his warm chest. "That's why I'm here, Henry."

"How old are you?" He asked, his brow furrowing slightly. A formality. I could sense his cock stiffening in his gym shorts.

"Nobody under eighteen allowed, here, right Henry?" I smiled, winking at him. "And it was my birthday yesterday."

"Then come with me." Shroud leaned in and whispered into my ear. His breath was hot and I could feel his desire.

He led me quietly to the door, checking the hall before bringing me out of the locker room. Down the short hall were the steam rooms and saunas, and it was toward a private sauna room we hurried. Sliding the sign on the door to occupied, he allowed me in. It smelled of warm cedar, old stone and fresh steam. When the door closed behind us he surveyed me. I knew I was prize, a girl to be taken, conquered and enjoyed. That's exactly what I wanted right now, to feel for a long moment controlled by Henry Shroud. Why shouldn't he control me? He controlled thousands of lives, hundreds of companies. Why not one more girl? Submission is confidence, I told myself. Confidence that you know you're making the right choice, that you can trust this man with your body. Clare had agreed, that to lose power for a moment, but just a moment, was excitement really way. You just had to know you'd get it back. I took off my shirt to give Shroud a better view.

"I can see I was watching the wrong girl," he said, smiling and extending a hand to my breast. "You're soft, Larkin."

"Emia," I said.

"Well, Emia. You're a good looking girl." He sat down on the cedar bench that ran the length of the wall. He squeezed one breast softly, his thumb brushing over the nipple as he began to trace my belly, his soft touch reaching my thigh. I shivered despite the heat. "Sit with me."

I did. I took a seat next to Shroud and let him stroke my thigh.

"Tell me about yourself," he said. Shroud smiled, squeezing my thigh and slipping his cool fingers under the fabric of my shorts. "I want to know more about this girl who's chasing after me."

"I just graduated this spring," I said. "From Kingstown Academy in Pennsylvania."

"I know it," he said, cracking up. "You know I went to Weston Prep? I guess we're rivals." A rivalry didn't stop his hand as he caressed my inner thigh. "Kiss me."

"I'd love to," I said. I'd never kissed a man with a beard before. What would it feel like? The hair on his cheek was soft, and his lips were warm. He traced the contours of my mouth with a gentle tongue, and I felt welcomed. It was easy to forget this man was forbidden to me. His mouth was careful on mine: tender and slow. When he pulled back to look at me I smiled, and leaned in for another kiss at once. I clasped his shoulder, and he encircled my waist with an arm. "Thank you," I said.

Shroud removed the cap of a bottle he'd brought with him, splashing water over the hot stones in the sauna and filling the room with a burst of steam. For a moment, I couldn't see, and in that brief second I felt his mouth on my breast, sucking and licking my hard left nipple, and circling my soft breast. Blood rushed to my cheeks. I was really doing this.

"I like that," I said, resting a hand on his head as he sucked at my breast, placing another on his back and stroking softly. It was almost romantic, but I knew this was just pleasure for both of us. Temporary, raw, carnal pleasure. After another moment he lifted his head. We were both beginning to sweat in the incredible heat, and I grew lightheaded.

"You're turn," he said, smiling at me as he placed my hands on his waistband. "Show me what you're made of, Emia Larkin."

I slid to the floor, kneeling in front of Darkwall's confident CEO and smelling his powerful musk mixing with the sauna's cedar.

"Like this?" I asked, blinking my eyelashes slowly and tugging on his shorts. He lifted himself slightly, and the shorts came off in my hands, sliding down his legs and revealing Shroud's hard cock. "Ooh!" I sighed, and he smiled proudly.

"Yes," he said. "Just like that."

I reached for his shaft hesitantly. His eyes coaxed me on. His veins throbbed visibly, and I could feel my own heartbeat flutter in my chest. I was nervous. I'd never been with a man like him before, poised and experienced and powerful. Around his groin was shaved smooth, unlike his chin, and the full uninterrupted length of his cock confronted me, begging to be sucked. A small tear of precum dripped from the head; he wanted me.

"It's so big," I said, gaping. My lips tingled..

"See how it tastes, Larkin girl."

My being a Larkin seemed to turn him on. Forbidden fruit tastes the sweetest.

Topless and still wearing only my shorts, I leaned in to his thighs, resting my arms on his powerful muscular legs and breathing in the steamy scent of Henry Shroud. Wrapping a hand around his cock I gauged its power, exhaling involuntarily at the feeling, the weight of it in my palm. I kissed the soft tip, the taste of his sweet precum luring me in. In a moment the head of his hard cock was between my lips, and I traced his shape with my tongue. He sighed, the tickle of my mouth new and unfamiliar.

Shroud took my head in his hand, lacing his fingers through my dark hair.

"Yes, Emia," he said softly, helping me take his full hot length into my mouth. His cock was smooth, the skin so soft yet the shaft so firm. I almost gurgled, trying to speak, murmuring into his cock and trying to meet his eyes. He moved my head for me, and I followed his rhythm, losing myself to his hand and his desire. Losing control. Shroud took me how he wanted me, his hard shaft gliding in and out of my mouth, his soft tip brushing against the back of my throat. I sucked diligently, trying to impress him, gripping the base of his cock and moving to the same pattern. With my free hand I reached for his balls, feeling their fragile firmness between my fingers, making him sigh in sweet hot agony.

"Old Larkin doesn't want you doing this, does he?" Shroud moaned. "He doesn't want you talking to me at all?"

"Mhnm," I replied, his cock blocking my murmur.

"You'll be in a lot of trouble, Larkin girl." He smiled, moving my mouth along his cock rapidly now. "You're a slut, you know that? Naughty Larkin slut."

"Mhm," I moaned into his cock again.

"Oh! Yes," he sighed, exhaling and arching his back instinctively. "Oh, you're *good*."

I pushed back forcefully against his hand, Shroud's cock falling from my mouth as I took in a deep breath. I breathed in again, the heat of the moment rolling through me, the freedom in my mouth marvelous for a moment. He tasted so good, sweet, manly. I couldn't resist his allure, or his strength. I had given myself over, and I couldn't go back. Nervousness had been replaced with blind passion.

"Henry?" I looked up at him from between his knees. Shroud met my eyes, his pupils dilated, black and round — he was enraptured. "Will you fuck me?"

"Climb up here, gorgeous," he said softly, patting his lap.

I stood, stepping slowly from my shorts. Shroud's eyes lingered on my black panties. Meeting his eyes I came forward, placing myself on his lap, his hard cock pressed against the outline of my pussy and extending up over my belly. I could feel the warm pulsing of his shaft as I kissed him, his heartbeat all around me, joining mine in thumping rhythm.

"Do you want me?" I asked in a whisper, furrowing my brows in mock worry and stroking the length of his erect cock with one hand.

"Oh, yes," he said, kissing me again. His soft beard brushed my cheek, tickling me and sending electricity dancing across my skin in the steamy air. He tugged at my panties. "Why don't you take these off, then?"

"Are you sure?" I asked again. "My father might be *very* angry with you."

"That's not exactly my problem, is it princess?" He replied, smiling greedily.

"Oh," I said, moving the band of fabric that covered my wet, craving pussy aside. "Is this?" I raised myself, kneeling on the bench over his lap to accommodate the length of his massive cock. As his tip breached my labia, slipping into my dripping pussy, I threw my head back in a long moan. He let out a sigh, too, gripping my hips with unbridled desire, pulling me down on his long cock, eager to fill me completely.

"Oh, God, yes," Shroud moaned. "Fuck."

One long, hot, wet moment later he was fully inside me. I clenched around him, but he was too big, pressing me open. My eyes had grown wide with shock and I met his, glowing with pride and pleasure. He must have seen this look on women before, the utter surprise at the feeling of his massive, hard cock spreading them open. I was only his latest conquest, his newest prize.

"How does it feel," he whispered, pulling me closer by the hips.

"It's too much," I managed. I breathed heavily, adjusting to him, my lips parting and my brows furrowing slightly in ecstasy. "Too big. Henry. You're too big."

"You'll get used to me," he said, smiling. Slowly he lifted me, raising me halfway off his throbbing shaft and brought me back down hard on his full length, forcing a cry from my throat as he pressed me open.

"See?" He asked softly. "It gets easier, Larkin girl. Now kiss me while I fuck you senseless. Come here."

I could hardly think as our lips met, fire beating through my veins as he moved my body on his cock, spreading my legs wide around him and bouncing me on his long hard cock. His tongue caressed my lips and I moaned heavily into him, closing my eyes and letting Shroud take control and take my body. It was intense, in the heat, the steam billowing around us and making me forget myself, blinding me to anything but the moment and his throbbing shaft inside my pussy. Our bodies made a soft clapping sound as they met in rhythm, my thighs hitting his, the base of his cock rubbing against my clit. He didn't release me from our kiss as he fucked me, warming me fully, moaning into me as I breathed hot and fast through my nose, almost unable to keep up.

In a moment he stood up with my legs still wrapped around his waist, his cock still buried in me. Our kiss didn't break as he hoisted me on his long shaft, pressing into me and moving my body up and down against his. My clit rubbed softly against him, and excited tendrils of electricity ran through my thighs and up my chest. My breasts brushed against his bare chest, tickling my sensitive nipples. I couldn't focus on one sensation. I was lost. My lips were warmed by his, my breasts were excited by his motion, my clit was electrified by the soft rush of his body against mine, and my pussy was taken fully by his infinite cock. I moaned constantly, the hum of our passion filling the steamy room, and the smell of our sex overwhelming even he graceful scent of cedar wood.

Before long it was too much, and I squirmed in his grasp, breaking the kiss and panting like the broken girl I was. He set me down on a higher bench, continuing his stroke slowly and methodically, slipping in and out of my drenched slit as if he owned it.

"Oh, my god Henry," I let out. "Fuck, you're so big. I can't think, Henry."

"Don't think," he replied. "Just let me take you."

I leaned back on my elbows, my eyes falling closed, and my skin tickled softly by the hot steam of the room. I was burning up, on fire from his powerful thrusts and tired by the hot sauna. It was all I could do to keep my legs open for him as he pounded me, gently and deeply. The meeting of our bodies made a quieter sound now that he had slowed, the sensation of each thrust taking a blissful eternity to reach my deepest core. With one hand I pressed on my clit, circling it carefully, rubbing myself in time with his cock.

"Cum for me, Emia. Let me hear you," Shroud whispered, his quiet words floating on the steam and softened by the sauna's wooden walls. "Let me hear how it feels to take my cock."

With that I let out the loud moans and yelps I'd been holding back, each breath coming sharp and musical, accompanying the sound of Shroud's hard thrusts. I yelped with each stroke, reaching to clutch his arm, squealing and sighing forcefully. The song of our breathing and our heartbeats merged in soft symphony and with my eyes closed all I could do was listen, feel the length of his cock reenter me again and again, pushing the walls of my eager pussy wide.

"Yes," he murmured. "Just like that Larkin girl."

"Mmm." I groaned, my clit tingling under my own touch. I could feel myself getting there, the rush inside me, and the impossible desire to clench all my muscles around

Shroud's hard cock. To pull him in as deep as he could be. I shook, the sauna appearing before me as my eyes flew open, the wave rolling through me from my core. My pussy ached, holding Shroud tightly as he fucked me through my orgasm, not stopping for my moans and shrieks and cries.

"Oh, yes, let me hear you, baby," he intoned, slipping his hard cock out of my pussy for a moment, my eyes watering and wanting him back. I couldn't speak. He filled me again, plunging into me hard. I felt him all the way inside me, pressing into my core, spreading me open. My climax broke and my hand fell away from my clit. I let out an overdue gasp. My eyes shut again, and I couldn't hold myself up. Falling against the warm wooden wall of the sauna I let him fuck me.

Shroud moaned deeply, and his cock pulsed with energy before he flooded my pussy with hot cum. Gripping me by the waist he pulled me tight to him, not wanting a sliver of his cock exposed as he filled me and came. I moaned, too, crying out and opening my eyes wide to watch him throw his head back and climax. The hot liquid inside me pressed around his cock, flowing from my pussy onto the sauna bench, dripping around us both.

"Come here," he said, exhaling heavily like a runner after a marathon. I obliged, and he lifted me to him. I held him around the chest as he pulled me up, turning us around and sitting so I was nestled into his lap, his cock still filling me. "Oh Emia, proud of yourself?"

"Oh," I said, still gasping for breath. "Yes, yes." I murmured softly into his chest and he wrapped me with his strong arms, kissing the top of my head.

We rested there for a moment, letting the heat and steam lull us in our wash of ecstasy, our desires quenched for now. He didn't let me go.

"Promise me one thing," I asked, eyes closed with my cheek still pressed to his chest. "Don't tell my dad."

"Oh I wouldn't dream of it," he chuckled. "That would ruin all the fun."

Maya K. Chase is a writer from Missouri who lives in Brooklyn. You can reach her at mayakchase@gmail.com and read her many other stories on Amazon.

www.ingramcontent.com/pod-product-compliance
Lightning Source LLC
Chambersburg PA
CBHW020341180726
47991CB00021B/2203